"Whaaaa—whoooaaaa!" I screamed as cold, bony fingers closed around my ankles. Then I felt my legs being tugged out from under me. I was being carried across my bedroom!

"Put me down!" I yelled.

My bedroom window slid open, all by itself.

"Hey," I croaked. If this was a dream, now was the time to wake up. But I didn't wake up.

Instead, I was thrown right out the window!

I screamed as the ground rushed up toward me. But just as I thought I was about to have a close encounter of the pain kind with the back patio, I stopped with a jerk. I was left swinging in the air, upside down—twenty feet above the ground. Buddy was still holding me by the ankles. And this was definitely *not* a dream!

Below me, the flagstone patio looked very hard and very far away.

Buddy dropped my left ankle, and I screamed again. The ground whooshed toward me. I flailed my arms, and I heard that horrible laugh again.

"You can't fly away, kid. So tell me, do you believe I'm a real ghost now or not?"

SHADOW ZONE™

THE GHOST OF CHICKEN LIVER HILL

BY J. R. BLACK

BULLSEYE BOOKS

Random House 🏠 New York

A BULLSEYE BOOK PUBLISHED BY RANDOM HOUSE, INC.

Library of Congress Catalog Card Number: 93-83966
ISBN: 0-679-85007-4
RL: 4.5

Manufactured in the United States of America   10 9 8 7 6 5 4 3 2 1

SHADOW ZONE is a trademark of Twelfth House Productions.

1

The Haunted Hill

It felt like I had a Sno-Cone in my boot instead of a foot. I couldn't feel my fingers. If I were in your freezer, you'd take me out and pour hot fudge sauce on me. For any of you slow learners out there, I was cold.

But I wasn't going home yet. Today was the day I was going to conquer Chicken Liver Hill. It was destiny. It was fate.

Or else it was stupid. I squinted through the thickening snow. There was only a narrow path all the way down to the bottom of the hill. Bushes and trees lined both sides. The prickly overgrown branches and brambles lurked in wait to snatch a scarf or scratch a cheek.

Maybe today *wasn't* the day to conquer Chicken Liver Hill. It looked even scarier than usual. And the slope was awfully icy. Most of the other sledders had gone home about a half hour ago. It was just too cold.

I twisted around for a second to see if Danielle Larkworthy and her best friend Katie Riggs were still around. I quickly turned back again when I spotted them throwing snowballs at each other. Now I'd *have* to take a run. I couldn't wimp out in front of girls.

Just then a hoot of stupid laughter floated across the cold air. "Hey, Toby-Wan Kenobi!"

Great. Things were really looking up. I knew who had called me without even turning around. Craig Rawley, Megaphone Mouth, the biggest bully in sixth grade. Craig could be counted on for two things: getting a D minus on every math test, and showing up just when you didn't want to see him.

Not that anybody ever wanted to see Craig Rawley except his buddies, Marty Lazar and Jeff Fingerhut. I closed my eyes and gripped my sled. "Just don't come over here," I muttered under my breath. "Please, please, please..."

"If it isn't Toby Bemus," Craig said, right by my elbow. "I'm surprised your mommy let you out today. It's gotta be below seventy degrees!"

Marty and Jeff gave grunts of stupid laughter. They were Craig Rawley's personal cheering section.

"Where's your knee-pads, Toby-Wan Kenobi?" Marty snickered. "And your helmet?"

I didn't answer them. My mother made me wear a helmet and knee-pads when I rode my bike. Big deal. I'd get the last laugh one day when one of those sleazoids crashed on his ten-speed. Hopefully into a speeding train.

"We're just in time to catch your run," Craig said. "So where are you going to roll off your sled? By the first bump, Chicken Liver?" Marty and Jeff started squawking like chickens, obviously thinking they were a riot.

"Maybe you should roll off *before* you start," Jeff said. "It'll save you time." The three goons laughed harder.

I ignored them and looked down the hill again. Chicken Liver Hill was only for the older kids and the daredevils. Sleds were dangerous on such a steep, narrow slope. Most kids just used large squares of cardboard.

The sheer drop made my stomach churn as I stared through the snow. It was straight down all the way except for a sharp turn to avoid an old fence that stuck out on the left side of the slope. And, worst of all, a huge, hundred-year-old elm lurked at the bottom.

On days when the snow and ice were just right, you went so fast that the only way to avoid the tree was to roll off your sled at the right time. Of course, all the kids tried to see

3

how long they could stay on the sled. Rolling off too soon counted as extremely sissy behavior.

There was even a grading system. If you rolled off at the very end of your ride, barely missing the tree, you were a Terminator. If you got past the part that always iced up, you were a Ninja. If you waited until you made the turn past the old fence, you were a Jellyfish. But if you rolled off at the first big bump, just over halfway down, you were a Yellow-Bellied Chicken Liver and got hooted off the hill.

Okay, I admit it. I was a Chicken Liver myself. But last week I'd almost made it to Jellyfish—until my sled had veered toward the fence. I'd heard lots of jeers as I rolled off and trudged back up the hill.

Today I would go farther. I just wished that elm tree didn't look so big and scary.

Its branches overhung the path, leaving the bottom of the hill in creepy shadows. It had a massive trunk with a chunk out of the side that faced Waterside Road. There was a curve in the road at exactly that spot, and one night about thirty years ago some high school kid had smashed into it in his '57 Chevy and died.

Jerks like Craig Rawley said that the guy's ghost haunted the spot. The story was that the ghost would force kids to stay on their sleds and

4

almost crash into the tree. But I wasn't afraid of ghosts.

I may be a coward, but I'm not crazy.

Craig, Marty, and Jeff made chicken noises again. The snow picked up and blew against my face. If those clowns hadn't been there, I definitely would have headed for home. Danielle and her friends had left, probably to get a round of hot chocolates at the diner. That sounded pretty good right now.

"Maybe he needs a push," Craig said as I got on my sled.

"But then he might go too fa-ast," Jeff said, drawing out the word in a whiny voice.

"Eat paste," I said. Even crashing into the elm tree would be better than staying there with Craig and his friends. I dug my toes in the snow and pushed off just as Craig gave me a shove.

The sled was off like a rocket. In a second, I was moving faster than Mr. Delaney, my homeroom teacher, after a spitball thrower. I heard Craig and his fellow goons jeering me, but all I could do was hold on. The thin skin of ice on top of the snow was slick and fast, fast, fast.

Bits of snow and ice pelted my face, and tears formed in my eyes. This was not fun. Not one bit. Between you and me, I was terrified.

Ka-bunk! I was over the first bump! I wasn't a

5

Chicken Liver, at least. I was in Jellyfish territory now. Snow flew in my eyes and I wondered if I could even *see* the old fence. But suddenly it loomed up out of the whiteness. I twisted the steering bar and cleared it by inches.

The snow was flying furiously now, and I could barely see. I was afraid to take my hands off the sled and wipe at my eyes. I knew I must be getting close to the tree, and the thought didn't calm my nerves. It was time to roll off! Even if I was still a Jellyfish, it was better than I'd ever done before.

Just then, I heard someone laugh. It sounded as though someone was *on* the sled with me. That's how close it was. I whipped my head around. Had Craig followed me? I couldn't see through the blinding snow. But Craig hadn't even had his sled with him today. It was probably the wind.

Then I heard it again. Actually, it wasn't a laugh. It was more like a snicker. And this time, I could have sworn I *felt* something. Something cold, like a chilly breath on my ear.

Ice stung my cheeks as the sled picked up even more speed. The tree appeared and disappeared through the swirling snow. It looked absolutely huge! It was time to roll off. It was *past* time. I was a Ninja now.

But I couldn't move. I was frozen to the sled! And I *felt* something, as though someone was on the sled with me, on top of me.

The shadows of the branches were like waving fingers, ready to clutch at me. The trunk loomed closer and closer. I was going to hit it!

Just then, I felt a mighty push, as though someone had picked me up and thrown me off the sled. I was flying through the air, then landing and rolling down the hill. I slid down to the very bottom and landed in some bushes. As I lay there, panting, my sled crashed into the elm.

I felt like a bug, lying on my back. I tried to get up, but I felt dizzy.

And then I heard it again. *Laughing.*

A chill ran down my spine. There was definitely *nobody* around. I peered up into the snarled branches overhead. All I saw were shadows and snow. The spooky laughter got louder, surrounding me.

Fear trickled down my neck along with melting snow. I tried to get up again but slipped and fell. Wiping snow from my eyes, I stared through the blowing flakes. All I could see was white.

"Who's there?" I called. My voice sounded shaky. "Who is it?"

But now I only heard the wind.

2

Burglars!

The wind. It had definitely been the wind, I told myself as I trudged home. My sled trailed behind me like the mocking laughter on the hill.

Craig, Marty, and Jeff hadn't believed me when I'd told them I made it to Terminator. The snow had been blowing too hard for them to see. "Once a Chicken Liver, always a Chicken Liver," Craig sang.

Actually, even *I* wasn't sure I'd made it all the way to Terminator. The end of the ride had been a blur. But still, I'd probably made it farther than Craig and his buddies ever had.

Why should I care what Craig thought, anyway? I put my sled in the garage and headed for the back porch. Craig Rawley was a bully and a big jerk. He thought it was cool to pretend to throw up on girls. He wore wrist weights just to walk around school. I stamped the snow off my boots, wishing that Craig Rawley were underneath them.

Even my mom didn't like Craig. She was always warning me to stay away from him. I think she was afraid he'd beat me to a pulp one day. She'd look guilty after telling me to avoid him, as if she hadn't meant to suggest I was a wimp. She was sensitive about that, since I didn't have a dad around. She was always offering to play catch or one-on-one. She had a wicked hook shot, too.

"Don't worry about being small," she kept saying. "You're the smartest boy in sixth grade."

Maybe, Mom. The only thing I knew for sure was that I was the smartest *shrimp* in sixth grade.

I left my boots on the back porch and went into the kitchen in my stocking feet. I knew better than to complain to my mother about Craig. She'd just worry. It was her favorite pastime.

Even though she wore jeans and cowboy boots, my mom was much older than most mothers. My best friend Brian Gardellis's mom looked like a kid next to her. I think his grandmother was only a little older than my mom. Mom didn't have me until she was thirty-six.

Not only was she pretty old, she was divorced. I don't remember my dad much at all, except that he was tall and skinny and quiet. He owned the hardware store in town and never did anything surprising in his life. That is, until he ran away with Belinda Welliver, a waitress at the diner. They live in San Diego now. I get a birthday card from him every year in Belinda's handwriting.

I was four years old when Dad left. It sounds terrible to say, but I don't miss him much. I guess he never spent much time with me when he was around.

My dad had cleaned out the savings account when he left. Ever since, Mom had held down two jobs. During the day, she sold real estate. Three nights a week, she taught ceramics at a nearby college. Our house was full of Mom's "creations." If you came downstairs at night and didn't turn on the lights, the lumpy pots and vases were pretty scary.

Now she had started to take classes at the college for her master's degree. She was hoping to get hired as a regular teacher in a few years, and then my college tuition would be free. Since I was only in sixth grade, this was pretty far away. Sometimes Mom spent too much time looking ahead. Pretty soon she'd be planning my retirement.

"That you, Toby?" Mom walked into the kitchen wearing her coat. "You're soaked!" she exclaimed.

"That's what happens when you go sledding, Mom," I said patiently.

I have to explain one more thing about my mom. She was a fusser. I was always wearing one more sweater than the other kids. Or on the first warm spring day, I was always the kid who'd still be wearing a wool hat and gloves. No wonder everyone thought I was a nerd.

"Mmmm, well, you'd better change into dry clothes. Did you have fun? Was Brian with you?"

"I had an okay time, but Brian wasn't there," I said, reaching for a cookie. "He had to go to some concert his sister was in."

Mom peered at me. "You mean you were alone?"

I munched on the cookie. "There were other kids on the hill, Mom."

"Okay. Listen, sweetie, I have to go. I've got a committee meeting for the Tilson Corners Winter Festival." Mom made a face. "If Elsie Toomer has her way, the color scheme will be orange and green this year. They're her favorite colors."

"Gross," I said. Elsie Toomer was a ditzy lady. Just because she was married to the chief of police, she thought it was her job to run the town.

Mom checked her purse for her keys. "Dinner will be a little late. What will you do until I get back, sweetie?"

I shrugged. "Watch a video, play Nintendo."

Mom sighed. "Why don't you try a book?"

I gasped. "Oh, no, don't make me! Not that! Anything but that! Not a...a *book!*"

"Toby Bernard Bemus, you are a monster." Mom grinned, then leaned over and kissed me. "I'm making chicken enchiladas for dinner."

"Great," I said. Mexican food—things were looking up!

"And clean your room!" Mom called as I climbed the stairs.

What can I say? It never lasts.

The wind was howling outside and the snow started to fall again. One thing about living in Vermont, you have to like snow.

It was getting dark, so I switched on a couple of lights. My room was cluttered with dirty socks and T-shirts as well as piles of books, videotapes, and CDs. What I needed was the Young Ruffians to inspire me. I popped the CD into the player, and the first Ruffians cut blasted out of the speakers. I picked up a pair of socks. Then I set up my hamper by the door and began to toss my dirty socks across the room.

"Two points, all *right!*" I called as a pair of yellow wool socks swished in.

Then suddenly the music changed into these weird sounds. It wasn't music, exactly. It sounded like tunes an alien with a tin ear might play. Covering my ears, I raced to the CD player. Maybe it wasn't tracking right.

When I pushed "stop," nothing happened. I pressed it again, but the weird sounds kept going. Whatever this stuff was, it skittered and moaned and set my teeth on edge. This was even worse than Deborah Pitowski's violin solo in music class!

I dropped to my hands and knees and reached for the plug. What a time for my CD player to go on the fritz. It was practically brand-new, and Mom had saved up for months to buy it. I pulled the plug and the sound stopped. *Whew.* I balled up a sweatshirt and tossed it toward the hamper.

It swished in—two points! But I didn't get to enjoy it, because all of a sudden the lights went out. I stood in the darkness for a minute, listening. I'm not a kid anymore, but I'm still not crazy about being alone in my house with no lights. I felt my way to the wall switch and clicked it. Nothing.

"Terrific," I mumbled.

Just then music blared out from the speakers downstairs, making me jump. I didn't recognize the song, but I did recognize the voice. It was Elvis Presley. Mom had a bunch of his old records. Had Mom come home early and cranked up "Don't Be Cruel"? It wasn't likely. Something else was going on. Something I didn't want to think about. Something terrifying.

Somebody was in the house.

3

I Meet a Ghost

My heart went *boom* against my ribs. Should I run down the stairs and risk bumping into a burglar? Or should I hide under the bed?

Before I could decide what cowardly thing to do, my sweatshirt hit me in the face. The sweatshirt that I'd just tossed in the hamper.

Someone was in the room!

I screamed.

And then I heard it again—*laughing*.

The hairs on my arms rose as I felt something cold against the back of my neck. I didn't move. I felt frozen, just as frozen as I'd been on the hill.

I heard the wind howling around the house and told myself to run. But my feet felt like somebody had nailed them to the carpet.

"Whatsa matter, kid?" The voice was low and right behind me. "Don't you like the King? I thought everybody was an Elvis fan."

"W-who are you?" My voice shook. I was afraid to turn around. "How'd you get in here?"

"Calm down, kid. Which question you want I should answer first?" The laughter came again, making my skin crawl. "Why doncha turn around? You scared of little old me?"

I was scared, but I turned around anyway. By now, my eyes had adjusted a bit. I didn't really *want* to look, but I did. I squinted through the darkness toward the figure across the room.

A teenager in a black leather jacket was leaning against my desk. He was cleaning his fingernails with a match. He waved it at me. "Greetings."

"W-who?" I could barely talk. Had this guy climbed in the window when my back was turned? Or had he sneaked up the stairs? How did he get in? My mom never forgot to lock the door.

"Name's Buddy. Pleased ta meetcha. What's your moniker, dad?"

"My what?"

Buddy snapped his fingers. "Name."

"Toby."

Buddy whistled. "Poor kid."

Who was this guy? An Elvis impersonator? He was dressed in a motorcycle jacket, a white T-shirt, and baggy jeans. He wore battered loafers and white socks. And his hair! It was combed straight back on the sides but poufed up in front. One curl hung down in the middle of his forehead.

He doesn't sound scary, I know. But believe me, he was. You had to see his eyes. They were the coldest eyes I'd ever seen. They were as gray as gravestones. And his skin was dead white.

"What do you want?" I asked, backing up a little. "My dad's downstairs."

Buddy checked his nails. "You ain't got a dad, dad. Don't bother lying. I know all. I don't know how I know, but I know. Which is weird, considering." He looked at the match a minute, and it flared into flame.

I stared at it. He hadn't struck the match against anything. Or had he?

"C-considering what?" I asked.

Buddy blew out the match. "Considering what a dumbbell I was when I was alive. A real brain drain."

"When you...you were...*alive?*"

Buddy spread his hands modestly. "I'm a whadd-ya-call-it, a poltergeist. Commonly called a ghost." He smiled a smile that chilled me all the way down to my toes. "And I'm haunting *you,* kid."

I backed away and hit the bed. I sank down on it. My whole body was shaking. "I don't believe you," I said.

"Didn't you ever hear of Buddy Parker? Geez, I thought I was famous. It isn't everybody who connects with that old elm in such a big way." Buddy clapped his hands together. "Whammo!"

"You mean *you're* the ghost of Chicken Liver Hill?" Now I knew the guy was lying. He probably got his kicks from breaking into houses and scaring kids. But why was he so pale? His skin glowed eerily across the room, as white as ashes.

"You shoulda been there that night. I was going fifty-five around that last curve. The next thing I know, I'm hugging a tree kissing the bark—and it's Johnny Angel time."

"Angel?" I said. Okay, so he was trying to scare me into thinking he was a ghost. But an angel? There was no way that *this* guy was from heaven.

Buddy looked annoyed. "So I went somewheres else. You ever been in detention, kid?"

When I didn't answer right away, Buddy rolled his eyes. "Whoa, I guess not. You're one of those whiny momma's boys, right?"

"You're just trying to scare me," I said shakily. "And it won't work." Of course, it *was*

18

working. "Just steal what you want and get out."

"You still don't believe me, do you, kid? You think I'm just some hood, right? I'm no hood." Buddy paused. "Well, not exactly. But now I'm a ghost, so show a little respect."

Buddy slid off the desk, and I shrank back. He headed toward me slowly. He seemed all bones inside his clothes. His pale, pale eyes were like stones sunk in his face.

"You don't believe your ears, do ya, kid? And you didn't on the hill, either. Who do you think threw you off that sled? You could've crashed into that tree. And take it from me, that smarts."

"You weren't there," I said.

Buddy snapped his fingers, and suddenly he was gone. *Vanished!* Then I saw the hamper rise up into the air, all by itself. It overturned, and all my dirty clothes fell out.

"P.U." Buddy's voice floated down from the ceiling. "Doncha ever do your laundry, kid?"

Next, the CD player drawer opened. The CD sailed like a Frisbee across the room. I ducked as more CDs whizzed over my head. A piece of paper floated over my desk and was torn to pieces.

"Hey!" I yelled. "That was my math homework!"

Suddenly Buddy was there again, standing

right in front of me. He grinned, and I saw that his gums were white. "You believe me now, kid?"

I stood up shakily. "I'm dreaming this!" I shouted. "You aren't real!" I said the words loud so that I would wake myself up.

Buddy's gruesome grin widened until it stretched across his face. "Oh, yeah? I'm your worst nightmare." Then he disappeared again.

"Whaaaa—whoooaaaa!" I screamed as cold, bony fingers closed around my ankles. Then I felt my legs being tugged out from under me, and I found myself hanging upside down. I was being carried across my bedroom by my ankles!

"Put me down!" I yelled. "Put me—"

But I stopped as my bedroom window slid open, all by itself. The cold winter wind rushed in. It blew the curtains in my face and rattled the shade.

"Hey," I croaked. If this was a dream, now was the time to wake up. But I didn't wake up.

Instead, I was thrown right out the window!

4

Hanging with a Ghoul

I screamed as the ground rushed up toward me.
But just as I thought I was about to have a close
encounter of the pain kind with the back patio, I
stopped with a jerk. I was left swinging in the
air, upside down—twenty feet above the ground.
Buddy was still holding me by the ankles. And
this was definitely *not* a dream!

Bits of hail stung my face, and the wind cut
through my sweatshirt. Below me, the flagstone
patio looked very hard and very far away. The
big maple in the backyard looked like it was
floating against the sky. Far below, I saw my
neighbor's clumsy sheepdog, Sweetie Pie, clamber
over our back fence and start sniffing near
our garbage.

Buddy dropped my left ankle, and I screamed
again. The ground whooshed toward me. I
flailed my arms, and I heard that horrible laugh
again.

"You can't fly away, kid. So tell me, do you believe I'm a real ghost now or not?"

"I believe! I believe!" I yelled. There was a lump in my throat, and my heart was hammering. I swung back and slapped up against the side of the house. I tried to hold on to the stucco, but I scraped my knuckles instead.

"Smart kid." Just as quickly as I'd been dropped out the window, I was hauled up again like a sack of potatoes. In another instant, I was dumped on the floor of my bedroom. I lay there, panting as hard as Sweetie Pie chasing the mailman. I wanted to kiss the carpet. Safe at last!

But then Buddy reappeared again. His wide, white-gummed grin made shivers run down my spine. I had a feeling that I wouldn't know what "safe" was for a very long time.

"Miss me?" Buddy asked.

I gulped. "Okay, I believe in you. Now, what do you want?"

Through the darkness, Buddy's cold eyes began to glow red. I wondered where he had really come from.

Just then the window slammed down again. All by itself.

"I just want a little assistance, kid," Buddy said.

"Assistance?"

Buddy snapped his fingers, and the lights came on again. I thought that having lights would make me feel less scared. But it didn't. Now I could really see how cold and gray Buddy looked. *Like a walking, talking corpse.*

"It's a funny thing," Buddy said. "There I am, in—uh, detention. Just hanging out, right? Only something ain't right. At first, it's just a nagging feeling. Then it's like a burning thing in my stomach. And then..." Buddy paused, and his eyes seemed to glow red again. "It gets worse. Much worse. And I know I gotta bust out. I gotta come back here and make things right."

"What things?"

"Somebody isn't letting me rest in peace, kid. I gotta find them."

"Who?"

Buddy shrugged. "That part I'm not so sure about. But you're going to help me."

"Me?" The biggest nerd in sixth grade? "Why me?"

"I've been watching the kids on the hill. Most of them are brain drains, like me. You got smarts."

"What am *I* supposed to do?" I asked. "I'm just a kid."

"I know," Buddy said. "But you got an edge—me. Look, this is serious, kid. I had no brakes

when I went down that hill. And I didn't discon-
nect my own brake cable. You got me?"

"Wait a second," I said. "Are you telling me
somebody *murdered* you?"

Buddy took a step toward me. I shrank back
against the wall. His face looked grim and evil.
"Everybody thinks I committed suicide. But I
didn't want to check out. You got me? Now I
can't rest until I make things right."

Slowly, what Buddy was saying sank in.
"You're asking me to help you catch your *murderer?*" I asked in disbelief.

"I'm not asking," Buddy said. "You got me?"

"But you died thirty years ago!"

"Twenty-nine."

"And it could be dangerous!" I pointed out.

Suddenly Buddy disappeared again. I
watched my English composition float off the
desk. It drifted across the room and hung over
my head.

"Wait a sec—" I started. But the paper
was torn into tiny little pieces right over my
head. They drifted down over me like
snowflakes.

The voice was low and nasty and right by
my ear. "Too dangerous, you said? Need some
more fresh air to make up your mind, kid?"

Slowly, very slowly, the window started to

rise again. All by itself, naturally. Or should I say *un*naturally.

I sat on my hands so they'd stop shaking. I swallowed hard. "Uh, actually, I'd be very glad to help out," I said.

When I woke up the next morning, there was no sign of Buddy. My window was shut. My CD player was plugged in. And all my clothes were in my hamper. I lay in bed and yawned. It had been a dream, I told myself. A nightmare. What kind of crazy person believed in ghosts?

Now that I had my head on straight again, I decided to turn over a new leaf in general. Today, I'd set a world record. A personal best for old Toby Bemus. I would get to school on time. I pulled on my clothes and ran downstairs for breakfast.

"Good morning, sleepyhead," Mom said. She was drinking coffee at the kitchen table, already dressed for work. "You were out like a light last night when I got home. I just let you sleep. All that sledding must have tired you out."

"Mmmmfff." My mouth was full of cereal. I wasn't about to tell Mom about my dream. She'd probably never let me near Chicken Liver Hill again.

"Don't gulp your food, Toby," Mom said as

she studied the newspaper. She has eyes in the back of her head. "You have plenty of time, for once."

But I had finished breakfast and was almost ready to go in five minutes. Mom kissed me good-bye on her way out. I went upstairs to get my knapsack. I slid my books into it and then reached for the homework I'd finished on Saturday. That's when I started to feel weird. I couldn't find my math homework *or* my English composition anywhere.

I was scared for a minute. But then I realized that I'd probably dreamed doing my homework, too!

Feeling better, I started off for school. Even getting in trouble with Mr. Delaney was better than the nightmare I'd had last night. I walked down the driveway, taking a deep breath of frosty air. Brian would be surprised when I met him at the corner on time. I liked to sleep late, and he usually had to wait for me. But if I was too late, he'd go on ahead to school.

Then a cold wind blew around my ankles, and I heard a creepy snicker.

"Morning, daddy-o."

5

Today's Lesson: B and E

I must have jumped ten feet in the air. I hadn't seen him at all. But there he was, leaning against the pine tree at the end of the driveway—Buddy, my personal nightmare.

He waved. "Wasn't a dream, bub, sorry."

"Go away," I whispered fiercely. "I'm on my way to school."

Slowly, Buddy shook his head.

"I'm supposed to meet my friend."

Buddy shook his head again.

"Buddy," I said desperately, "I'm a kid. Kids go to school. There's no way out of it. Believe me, I've considered the options."

"Don't be a scaredy-cat. Just cut."

"Cut?"

"C-u-t," Buddy spelled out. "We got business this morning. Follow me."

I hesitated. But then I saw myself dangling by my heels from the top of the pine tree. I was supposed to be a smart kid, right? So what did I do? I'll give you one guess.

"Good choice," Buddy said approvingly as I trotted after him. Then he disappeared.

"Don't get any ideas, kid." His voice was over me, as though he were walking beside me. "I just don't want to attract attention."

"Then don't talk," I said out of the corner of my mouth as Mrs. Andover, my neighbor, waved from her lawn. She picked up the paper and started back inside, hopping across the snow in her slippers. Sweetie Pie pressed her hairy head against the fence as we walked by.

The sun was out today, but it was like I was walking in a bubble of freezing air. Why did ghosts have to be so *cold?*

I felt a tiny tug on my scarf. Buddy was pulling it to make me quicken my pace.

"Here's the plan, kid. We're going to check out our first suspect. My best friend—at least I *thought* he was my best friend. He could take a car apart and put it back together in ten seconds flat."

"So he could have cut your brake line," I said.

"Exacto-rama, kid. The only thing is, Ray was a stand-up guy. True blue, ya know? We were buddies, womb to tomb."

"If he was such a great guy, why is he a suspect?" I asked.

Buddy didn't answer for a minute. Then he said, "I always thought that Ray was sweet on my girl, Chi Chi. She was a real tomato, if you catch my drift...I mean, she was a very nice girl. You shoulda seen her teasing her hair and snapping her gum and singing along with the Shirelles. All at the same time!"

"Wow," I said. "I bet she was in the gifted program at school, too."

"Whoa, a wise guy. Chi Chi had smarts, too. Anyway, I thought you could nose around and find out some stuff about Ray."

"Tilson Corners is a small town, but I don't know everybody," I said. "What's his last name?"

"Ebsen."

"Ebsen? Ray *Ebsen*?" I stopped in my tracks. "Forget it!"

"What do you mean, forget it?" Buddy's voice lowered. "He didn't make like a frog and croak, did he?"

"Huh?"

A chilly sigh drifted past my ear. "Did anyone ever tell you that you're a real L-seven, kid?"

"A what?"

Suddenly Buddy's hands appeared in front of

my eyes. I mean, *only* his hands. It was totally weird. One hand made an L shape with his thumb and forefinger. The other hand made the same shape upside down so it looked like a 7. Then he fitted his fingers together to make a square.

"I get it," I said with a sigh. "A square. A nerd. A dweeb. Believe me, I've heard it all before."

Buddy's hands disappeared. "Back to Ray. Is he still alive, or what?"

I shivered. "He's alive, all right. He runs the gas station over on Route 16. He lives in this gross place out back."

"Good. You lead."

"Listen to me, Buddy." I was getting desperate. "Ray Ebsen's been in jail. He robbed the diner in the next town ten years ago. He has a million tattoos. Not to mention a bulldog who likes to chew nails."

Buddy whistled. "Ray always said he'd make a name for himself in this town. You gotta give the guy credit."

"He's mean, Buddy," I said. "Everybody's scared of him."

"So? I'm not." Buddy chuckled. "What can he do to me? I'm already dead."

"I'm not," I pointed out. "So far."

"You worry too much, kid. Get a move on.

30

It's time for a little B and E."

"L-seven, B and E," I grumbled. "I think I need a ghost codebook."

"B and E is breaking and entering, kid."

"As in burglary? Robbery? Theft?" My voice squeaked out. I planted my feet on the sidewalk. "No way."

Buddy tugged on my scarf, but I didn't budge.

"You're not going to steal anything, you nervous Nellie," Buddy said. "You're just going to look around."

"No way." It was one thing to be haunted. But to be haunted by a ghost who wanted to turn you into a criminal was too much. I didn't want to be the one walking around with cold eyes and no blood in my veins. I didn't want to end up a ghost myself.

But then my scarf pulled taut, and I was yanked forward, choking.

"Change your mind?" Buddy asked.

It was either keep walking or stop breathing. I couldn't get air into my lungs. "Okay!" I choked. The pressure let up a little bit.

I took a shaky breath. I was about to break into the house of an ex-con with a bulldog and a hair-trigger temper. Would Ray Ebsen believe me if I told him his best friend's ghost made me do it?

31

6

Toby Bemus:
America's Most Wanted

I took a shortcut through Miller's Woods and came out on Route 16. That way, I didn't have to go through town. My mom's office is right on Main Street. If she saw me, I'd be dead meat.

Speaking of dead meat, I sure wished I had a steak to throw to Ray's dog, Killer. When I told Buddy the dog liked to chew nails, I hadn't been exaggerating.

"Whatsa matter, kid? You look kinda pale." Suddenly Buddy materialized next to me.

"You should talk," I muttered. Buddy looked even whiter today. And for the first time I noticed a faint unpleasant smell. Maybe it was a dead raccoon in the woods.

"Ray's a pussycat," Buddy said. "He's all bark and no bite."

"And what about Killer?" I asked. "He's all bite, if you ask me."

"I never met a pooch who didn't like me," Buddy said. "This will be no sweat. And just think, if you get the goods on Ray, I could be out of your hair by sundown."

"That's true," I said, cheering up.

"Well, you don't have to look so happy about it," Buddy said. "I thought we were getting to be friends."

Friends? He had to be kidding. But I didn't want to be strangled by my scarf, so I just said, "Shush! We're getting close."

The gas station was just around the next bend. Ray's house was behind it. We'd have to cut through the woods in back to circle around so that Ray didn't see us. If he wasn't fixing a car, he usually sat in a folding chair in front of the station. He never seemed to get much business. I guess people still didn't trust him much.

I left the road and snuck into the woods. That's when Buddy disappeared, the coward. Now, if Ray saw me, I was on my own. I inched forward toward the screen of bushes on one side of the station. I heard a radio playing, and Ray came out of the garage, wiping his fingers on a rag. Then he hit the side of the soda machine, and a can rattled down. He took the can back into the garage.

I looked into the side yard. Killer was now

tied up with a chain instead of a rope. That was a good sign.

"Did you see that belly? Ray sure got fat," Buddy said, right in my ear.

I jumped. "Do you mind? Your breath is freezing," I muttered.

"*I'm* freezing," Buddy complained. "It's cold being a ghost. You know, I can't believe Ray let himself go like that."

"He's practically fifty years old," I said. "And you don't look so hot yourself."

"Get a move on, will ya?" Buddy said. He sounded kind of irritated. He probably still saw himself as a handsome guy. Maybe I should introduce him to a mirror.

I crept back to the path and struck off for Ray's house. I felt better knowing Ray was busy working on a car.

I climbed the back fence and ran across the yard. Then I tried the back door. Locked. I didn't want to try the front door. All Ray had to do was look out the back window of the service station and he'd see me.

"Oh, well," I said. "I guess we can head back to town now. Maybe I can make third period."

"Hold on." Buddy's voice stopped me dead. I should have been used to it, but you try having a cold, spooky voice right at your ear when you least expect it.

A long metal pick floated in the air toward me. "Take it!" Buddy ordered.

I took it. It felt cold against my hand. I'd forgotten my gloves that morning. "What is it?"

"It's a pick," Buddy said. "Jimmy the lock."

"Jimmy who?"

Buddy sounded exasperated. "Just stick the little end into the lock and wiggle it around. That's right," he said as I followed his order. "Now grab the doorknob. Keep wiggling it, will ya? Easy. Easy..."

"This is stupid," I said. "I can't—"

But right then, I heard a click. I turned the knob, and the door opened, just like that. "Wow," I said. I had actually picked a lock! Now I was a full-fledged burglar.

"Hurry up, kid," Buddy urged.

I pushed open the door and peered into the kitchen. I tiptoed across the torn linoleum. Dishes were piled high in the sink. On the rickety kitchen table was a crusty plate and a cup of something with a thin skin of milk floating on the surface.

"Yuck," I said.

"Get a move on, bub," Buddy said. "Check out the bedroom."

"What am I looking for?" I asked.

"An ID bracelet," Buddy said. "With my name on it."

Kicking away a pair of socks, I started up the stairs. At the top, there were only two doors. One of them led to the bathroom, and the other to Ray's bedroom.

The bed was unmade, and laundry was piled in one corner. Stacks of auto magazines were scattered on either side of the bed. A plate with half an Oreo rested on one stack. Half a glass of sour-smelling milk was on the other. And I thought *I* was messy.

"Find out anything?" Buddy called from downstairs.

"Yeah," I called back. "Ray is a real slob."

I went over to the bureau against the wall. A bunch of keys and some change had been thrown on top. An old photograph was tucked into the mirror. I leaned over to peer at it.

It was a black-and-white photograph of a teenage girl. It wasn't really in focus, and the girl was turning her head so that her shiny blond hair swung against her cheeks. I couldn't see her face too well, but I could tell she was laughing.

Suddenly Buddy was there, looking over my shoulder. I almost jumped ten feet in the air.

"Will you stop *doing* that!"

"Chi Chi," Buddy said, shaking his head. "What a chick."

"What is Ray doing with an old picture of Chi Chi?" I said.

"See what I mean? He was sweet on her," Buddy said.

The top drawer of the dresser opened slowly. Socks and underwear began to fly out.

"Maybe it was because she could adjust the timing on an engine faster than you can sneeze," Buddy said as more clothes piled on the floor. "That really won Ray's heart."

"Why are you throwing Ray's clothes on the floor, Buddy?" I asked. "Not that he'll notice."

"I'm looking for the ID bracelet," Buddy said. "Help me out. Look in the next drawer."

I looked through the next drawer, but there was just a bunch of T-shirts that might have been white a couple of hundred years ago.

"There's nothing here," I said. "We might as well—" But before I could finish the sentence, Buddy disappeared. "Hey!" I said, my voice echoing in the empty room.

But in another second, I knew why Buddy had disappeared. I heard the sound of a key in the lock. Ray Ebsen was home.

Then I heard snuffling and snarling. Killer was home too!

7

Trapped!

"Buddy, help me!" I called in a frantic whisper.

A cold chuckle came from the air. "Sorry, kid. You're on your own."

The door opened downstairs, and I heard Killer snarling. Quickly I picked up the clothes on the floor and stuffed them back into the drawers. Luckily, Ray didn't believe in folding.

Ray's voice floated up the staircase. "Whatsa matter, boy? What's got into ya?"

He smells lunch, I thought with a shudder. I had to get out before I was dog food!

I couldn't go back downstairs. The house was too small. Ray would see me.

I looked around the room. There was a closet, but I could see that it was crammed with junk. Even if I managed to squeeze in and close the door, Killer would sniff me out like a bloodhound.

My only chance was if Killer and Ray stayed

downstairs. Then, as soon as they left for the gas station, I could sneak out the back door again.

It was a good plan...until I heard the click-click of Killer's toenails on the living room floor. My heart banged like the Young Ruffians' drum solo on "Born to Be Brave" when he barked up the stairs.

"Hey, boy!" Ray called. "Food in the kitchen. Killer! C'mere, pooch!"

I backed away until I hit the windowsill. Then I heard Killer pounding up the wood stairs!

Ray's impatient footsteps followed Killer. "You crazy pooch."

Any minute now, Killer would have me in a jaw-lock, and Ray Ebsen, ex-con, would be right behind him. I had to get out of there!

I glanced out the window. The backyard looked really far down. Why couldn't Buddy hang me outside the window until Killer and Ray left? But my head would probably hit the porch roof.

Porch roof?

In another second, I had pulled up the window. As Killer's toenails skittered down the short upstairs hall, I eased myself out and dropped as quietly as I could onto the porch roof.

Killer rounded the corner and raced into the bedroom just as I closed the window. Killer launched himself at the glass, and I saw his long, glistening teeth. I stuck out my tongue at him.

Then I turned and half-fell, half-slid my way down the slope of the porch roof. I grabbed the gutter and eased over the side. The gutter groaned a little, but it didn't break. I hung by my arms and let go, straight into a prickly bush.

I was scratched up, but I was alive. I peeked in the kitchen window as Ray walked back in. He went to a frying pan on the stove and flipped a grilled cheese sandwich that was charred on one side. His back was to me. It was now or never. I made a mad dash across the lawn.

I had almost reached the fence when I heard the back door open. I dived behind a tree.

"If you want to go out so much, then go!" Ray snapped at Killer. The door shut again.

Grrrrrr. The low growl made me break out in a cold sweat. I peeked around the tree. Killer was on the porch. The hair on his neck got all bristly as his small mean eyes met mine. With a snarl, he leaped off the porch and headed straight for me.

I didn't have time to think. Pure terror made my legs work. I ran for my life across the yard.

Twenty yards to go. Ten. I heard the sound of pounding paws behind me and the rasp of Killer's breath.

I hit the fence and started up it in one motion. My legs pumped and my fingers grabbed as Killer leaped against the fence, missing me by inches. I reached the top just as he jumped again. As I swung myself over, his teeth closed on the leg of my jeans. I heard the sound of material ripping as I fell over the fence.

Safe! Killer was barking and snarling and jumping at the fence in frustration. I got to my feet and hurried toward the woods.

Buddy was leaning against a tree, laughing his head off. "You gotta try out for the track team, kid," he said. "That was some hundred-yard dash."

My legs were still shaking. There was a huge tear in the leg of my jeans. My heart was still pounding, and I felt like I might throw up.

"What happened to you?" I demanded angrily. "You left me alone back there. I could have been ripped to pieces!"

Buddy examined his nails. "Aw, stop bellyaching. Time to split. That dog is giving me a headache."

He turned and started off down the path.

"You can't get a headache," I pointed out as

I followed him. "You're dead."

"Don't give me any lip, kid. We have work to do."

I followed him deeper into the woods. "I'm not going anywhere else with you," I yelled. "I'm going home before something *really* bad happens."

Buddy whirled around and looked at me. "I mean it," I said.

"You keep forgetting something, bub. You don't have a *choice.*"

"Oh, yeah?" I said. I tried to sound tough, like Craig Rawley. But my voice shook a little. I couldn't help it. Buddy's face was close, and I smelled that dead smell again. Patches of his skin were peeling. No, not peeling. *Rotting.*

"Yeah," Buddy said in a low menacing voice. "Or maybe you'd like to turn into something like this?"

Suddenly, instead of Buddy's face, I saw a skull. A skull with hollow sockets for eyes. There was a wide gaping hole where the mouth should be. And the hole was stretched wide in a horrible grin.

I couldn't run. I couldn't move.

I felt a bony hand on my shoulder. It *was* bone. It was the hand of a skeleton. I screamed.

Then Buddy was back with the same dead-white face and cold gravestone eyes. For once I was almost glad to see him. Better to see Buddy the ghost than Buddy the skeleton.

"You get my drift, kid?" Buddy asked. "You have no idea what I can do. So don't even *think* about trying to push me around."

I nodded. I couldn't talk.

"Now, let's head for town. I want to visit some of my old haunts." Buddy laughed, a horrible, croaking cackle.

We kept to the back roads and ended up on the north end of Main Street. Buddy disappeared, but if I stretched out my hand I could feel a cold vapor. The wind played with the flap of my torn jeans, sending a chill down my leg.

"Hey, these cars are cool. Whoa, hold the phone. What's that?" Buddy asked me. "That store there."

"It's a video store," I said. "You rent movies there to watch at home."

"What? Does everybody have a theater in their house? That's cool."

"No, you watch them on your TV," I explained.

"Why would anyone want to see movies on TV?" Buddy asked. "It's so *small*. And it's black and white."

"For a ghost who's been haunting the earth for thirty years, you're really out of touch," I said.

"Well, kid, my attention span's not too great."

Right then, old Mrs. Neidermeyer walked by and gave me a funny look. "Would you mind if I didn't talk to you?" I muttered to Buddy as soon as she had passed. "People will think I'm crazy."

"Let me give you a tip, kid. You worry too much. Who was that?"

"Old Mrs. Neidermeyer."

"Whoa. Stop my clock. Ophelia Neidermeyer? She taught me English. She was a dish."

"Mrs. *Neidermeyer*? You've got to be kidding." I blurted out the sentence before I had realized that T. C. Toomer, the chief of police, was writing out a ticket across the street. I scurried forward, glad he hadn't seen me. "Shhh," I said. "It's Chief Toomer."

"Toomer?" Buddy snickered. "Chief of police? I think I'm gonna bust a gut laughing."

I turned into the narrow alley that ran between Dawson's Bookshop and the dentist's office. Then I leaned against the brick wall and tried to look nonchalant. It wasn't easy.

I spoke to Buddy out of the corner of my mouth. "Look, I'm supposed to be in school. If anybody sees me, I'll be in big trouble."

"You worry too much," Buddy said in my ear.

"I'm cutting school. It's a small town. I'd be crazy *not* to worry."

"You're making me nervous, kid," Buddy said. "Relax. It's the secret to getting away with stuff."

Great. Now a ghost who could turn into a grinning skull is telling me to relax. Buddy pushed me from behind, and I almost fell onto the sidewalk. Fortunately, no one saw me.

"Okay, okay," I muttered. "But I can only go two more blocks. My mom works at 27 Main."

"Hey, who's your mom, anyway? Maybe I know her. Oops. *Knew* her."

But before I could answer Buddy, the door to the dentist's office opened and my homeroom teacher walked out.

I bolted back into the alley, but it was too late. Mr. Delaney had seen me!

8

Never Take a Ghoul to School

I waited all night for Mr. Delaney to call my mom to tell her I'd cut school. But the phone didn't ring. My mom sketched some lumpy ceramic vases she wanted to make, and I pretended to do my homework.

Buddy never showed up downstairs. For some reason, I never saw him in any other room in the house except mine. Lucky me.

Finally, it was time for bed. Mom kissed me good night at the door to my room. When I opened the door, she wrinkled her nose.

"I thought I told you to clean up in there," she said.

"I did," I protested.

"Well, put some elbow grease into it next time," Mom said. "Good night, lamb chop."

"*Mom—*"

"Oops, sorry. Good night, Toby. My big man." She gave me that goony smile that told me she thought I was adorable.

I sighed as I climbed into my pajamas. At least Buddy hadn't appeared again. I shut off the light and closed my eyes. You'd think I'd be too spooked to sleep, with a day full of ghosts and skulls and man-eating dogs, but I was exhausted.

"Sweet dreams, daddy-o."

My eyes flew open. The voice had come from underneath my bed. I hung over the edge upside down and met a pair of pale glowing eyes.

"Buddy!"

"Who else?"

"Are you going to stay there?"

"Where else?" Buddy stretched. "It's cold outside. Go to sleep. I've got a big day lined up for us tomorrow."

"I can't cut school tomorrow, too," I said desperately. "I'll get suspended. Mom will ground me, and I won't be able to help you at all."

"No problemo, kid. You're going to school."

"Good."

"And I'm coming with you."

Since I was hanging upside down, my hair was already standing on end. But believe me, it would have done the same thing if I'd been standing up. I was taking a ghoul to school!

The next morning Buddy walked to school with

me and Brian. Of course, Brian didn't *know* Buddy was with us. Every once in a while, Buddy would appear behind a tree ahead of us and wave at me. What a joker.

We turned onto Willow and passed a delivery truck. I saw Buddy leaning against it, his face turned away. Brian didn't even notice him. As we passed, Buddy gave me a little kick in the rear. I gasped and quickened my pace.

"Did you smell that?" Brian asked, wrinkling his nose. "Whew. Smells like a dead cat. Hey, what happened to you yesterday? Were you sick?"

"I cut," I said.

"You *cut*? I can't believe it." Brian shook his head. "I hope you forged a note for today."

"It won't help," I said. "Mr. Delaney saw me on Main Street yesterday. He knows I wasn't sick."

Brian whistled. "You're going to be dog meat."

I heard Buddy snicker. "You shoulda seen him yesterday."

Finally! Buddy talked! He couldn't resist opening his big mouth. "Did you hear that?" I asked Brian excitedly.

"Hear what?" Brian frowned, and the freckles on his face mashed together. Brian has more

48

freckles than anyone you've ever seen. He has orange hair that he's embarrassed about and skinny wrists he tries to hide by stretching out the sleeves of his sweaters. Looking at him you'd think he was a nerd. But he's smart and funny and loyal. What else do you need in a best friend?

If only he could hear ghosts, too.

"Oh, nothing," I said.

"He can't hear me," Buddy said. "Only you can. You're the lucky kid in the Shadow Zone."

I wanted to ask Buddy what he meant, but this wasn't the time or place. "Shut up," I grumbled.

"Huh?" Brian asked as we crossed Barn Road.

"Nothing."

"I don't get it," Brian said. "Why'd you cut school yesterday? What did you do?"

Buddy snickered. "Oh, just a little B and E."

"I just hung around," I said.

"Toby, I feel it's my duty as your best friend to let you know this," Brian said. "You are in excellent danger of seriously losing it."

"What do you mean?"

"You cut because you felt like it? And then you hung around?" Brian said in disbelief. "The least you could have done was have *fun*. Why didn't you go to see that new movie, *Nightmare Alley?*"

I have enough of that in real life. Before I could answer, the school came into view. My footsteps dragged.

"Nervous?" Brian asked. "Don't blame you."

"Don't be such a sissy," Buddy said.

"Maybe Mr. Delaney didn't see me after all," I said. "Maybe I just thought he did."

"Maybe," Brian said doubtfully.

Buddy just laughed.

"Mr. Bemus, may I see you for a moment?"

Mr. Delaney's face looked almost as scary as Buddy's. It didn't take a genius to figure out that he was not going to tell me I got an A on my last test.

He'd snagged me right outside the entrance. Brian gave me a nervous look as he scurried away. I sighed and turned to Mr. Delaney.

"Would you mind telling me what you were doing on Main Street yesterday when you were absent from school?" he asked.

"I was sick," I said. "Then I felt better, so I went downtown to tell my mom not to worry about me."

"I see," Mr. Delaney said. "Did you bring a note from your mother explaining your absence?"

"I had one," I said. "But I dropped it in the snow, and the ink ran."

"I see. Well, why don't we take a trip to the phone in Mr. Belson's office and give her a call?"

The game was up. I knew the chances of Mr. Delaney's buying the story were slim. But a kid owes it to himself to try.

Then I decided to tell the truth—sort of. "Mr. Delaney, you got me. I cut school yesterday. Didn't you ever need a day off?"

"All the time," Mr. Delaney said. "But I wait for Saturday. Those are the rules."

"But you were on Main Street yesterday," I pointed out.

Mr. Delaney looked annoyed. "I was having a root canal. Talk to me when your teeth start to go. Now come on."

"Mr. Delaney, wait," I said desperately. "If I promise never ever to cut school again, will you not call my mom? She's been kind of depressed and worried lately, and I really don't want to bother her." That wasn't really a lie. My mom was *usually* worried about something.

Mr. Delaney ran his hand through his hair. It was pretty thin. He had a bald spot developing in the back, too. But at least he didn't try to disguise it by combing his hair over it and spraying it until it looked like couch fabric.

I could see that what I said made him think. "I'm sorry to hear that Charlene—I mean, your mother—hasn't been doing well," he said in a soft voice. Then he clapped me on the shoulder. "Okay, I'll let you off the hook. Just this once."

"Thanks, Mr. Delaney," I said fervently. "You won't regret it. I promise." You've got to grovel when a teacher gives you a break.

Mr. Delaney headed into school. I let out the breath I'd been holding.

"What a wimp," Buddy said. "People could always snow Gerry."

"Be quiet," I whispered to Buddy. "You're always butting in."

Just then Craig Rawley appeared at my elbow. "Talking to yourself, Bemus?" he hooted.

Jeff Fingerhut gave his loud hyena laugh. "Who else would talk to him?"

"Want me to hang those guys off the school roof?" Buddy asked. "This time, I'll let go."

"No!" I blurted. Buddy had sounded totally serious. Then I realized that I had been yelling at thin air.

Craig, Jeff, and Marty eyed me curiously. Then they hooted with laughter and ran inside.

By lunchtime, the word was out all over school: Toby Bemus is bonkers!

9

My Day Gets Worse

After lunch that day, Brian and I went to the schoolyard. He was sticking close to me because so many of the kids kept staring at me and whispering. He just glared at them until they looked away.

"Craig Rawley is a nimrod," Brian said. "Want to shoot some hoops?"

"Nah," I said, distracted. Buddy wasn't around. I didn't feel his cold breath or smell that slightly rotten smell. Not that I *missed* him. But I couldn't help wondering what he was up to. Craig, Jeff, and Marty were playing soccer near the fence. Jeff tried to kick a goal, and it flew over Craig's head and bounced near me. I started to kick it back. But suddenly the ball moved by itself. It flew up into the air and zoomed toward Craig with incredible speed.

"Wow," Brian said, watching the ball. "I didn't know you could kick like—"

Brian stopped as the ball took a sudden dip and then hit Craig smack in the nose. Everyone around him burst out laughing, even Jeff and Marty. But they stopped as soon as Craig looked at them.

He scowled at me. Even across the distance, I could see I was in trouble.

"Uh-oh," Brian said.

"I'll get you for that, Toby Bemus!" Craig yelled. "Now I know you're crazy! Nobody messes with me and gets away with it!"

Buddy's chuckle froze my earlobe. "Guess that showed him."

"What's going on with you?" Brian asked me. "You're acting so weird. You used to be really scared of Craig. I mean," he said quickly, "you'd be stupid *not* to be scared of him. Everybody is, even the kids in seventh grade."

"Is this whole school full of wimps?" Buddy muttered.

I couldn't take one more second of Buddy's talking in my ear. It was like somebody had implanted a Walkman in my head with an obnoxious disc jockey.

"Will you leave me alone!" I burst out.

Brian looked hurt. "I was just asking."

"Not you, Brian," I said, frustrated. "I..."

"I just thought maybe something was wrong

54

or something," Brian mumbled.

"What are you bothering with this guy for, anyway?" Buddy said. "He's a wimp, too."

"Shut up!" I shouted. "Just shut up and get lost!"

Brian's hurt look slowly changed to disbelief, then anger. "Fine!" he shouted. "Fine with me!" He stomped off toward the basketball court.

"Whoa," Buddy said. "I didn't think you'd get rid of him that fast. If you ask me—"

"I didn't!" I shouted. A bunch of kids looked over at me, but I didn't care. How can my reputation get any worse? I thought as I plodded into school to wait in the gym for the bell.

When the bell rang, I filed into the classroom with the rest of the kids. I'd have to apologize to Brian later, when Buddy wasn't around.

We waited for Kiki Malone, the hall monitor, to hang up her coat in the cloakroom at the back of the classroom. She always waited until the very last student returned from recess. She took her job as hall monitor very seriously.

"Mr. Delaney!" Kiki stuck her head out of the cloakroom door. "You'd better come back here."

Frowning at the shaky note in Kiki's voice, Mr. Delaney hurried down the aisle. He stood in the doorway of the cloakroom and looked inside.

"Christopher Columbus!" he exclaimed. He

always said that when he was really exasperated or angry. You always knew he had substituted it for some expression we weren't allowed to hear.

A bunch of us got out of our seats and went to peek in the cloakroom door. Every single coat in the cloakroom had been turned inside out. I knew they were all on the wrong hooks because I could see my maroon down jacket way at the other end of the closet. The scarves were piled in the middle of the closet like spaghetti.

"Who did this?" Mr. Delaney demanded. His eyes roamed around the room slowly. His gaze rested on me for a fraction of a second while I tried not to look guilty.

"All right, class," he said. "Whoever did this had better confess. I'm not going to overlook this kind of malicious mischief!"

"Mr. Delaney?" Katie Riggs's mouth was open. She was staring over Mr. Delaney's shoulder with a horrified expression.

I whipped my head around. Had Buddy actually materialized in front of the sixth-grade class?

But Katie hadn't seen Buddy. The aquarium we'd started after the "Our Friends the Fish" chapter in our science textbook was overflowing with suds. They bubbled over the top and ran down to soak the floor. Somebody had put bubble bath in the aquarium!

Cissy Oppenheimer started to cry. "Herman!" she wailed. Herman was the name of the class's pet angelfish. She pointed at the tank. "He's dead!"

Sure enough, he was floating on the surface, almost hidden by the frothy bubbles. "He was my *friend*," Cissy blubbered loudly. Talk about crybabies. Cissy really lived up to her name.

But Cissy's tears started everyone talking at once. Everyone was exclaiming about Herman or wondering about who'd messed up the cloak-room. Everyone but me. I *knew* who'd done it.

"Oh, Herman!" Cissy sobbed. She dipped the little mesh basket into the aquarium and scooped him out. What was she going to do, give him mouth-to-mouth resuscitation?

"That's enough, class!" Mr. Delaney bellowed. His face was red. "Everyone sit down and be quiet!"

When Mr. Delaney raised his voice, he got in-stant obedience. Everyone shut up fast. Even Cissy dropped Herman back in the tank and ran to her seat. She stopped crying and only let out an occasional hiccup.

"That's better," Mr. Delaney said. "Now, I want the culprit to come forward immediately." Nobody said anything. "I mean *now*. Or else this class will stay after school *every day* until school ends until someone confesses!"

"Toby Bemus has been acting really weird," Craig said. What a pal.

"I saw him come back into school way before the bell," Marty Lazar said.

I sank a little lower in my seat.

"Well, Toby?" Mr. Delaney said.

"I was cold," I said. "I didn't do it."

His eyes bored into mine. I guess I looked a little guilty, because he frowned. But he looked away. "Toby denies the charge. Does anyone else have anything to—"

Danielle Larkworthy let out a little shriek. "Mr. Delaney!" she cried. "My sweater is missing!"

"Are you sure, Danielle?" Mr. Delaney asked.

"I'm positive. I left it right here, on the back of my chair, when I went to look in the cloakroom. It's new. I got it for my birthday," Danielle said. She looked really upset.

I didn't get it. Why would Buddy take Danielle Larkworthy's sweater? Sure, he kept complaining about being cold. But it would be way too small.

"I don't like this," Mr. Delaney said. "I don't like this at all. Does anyone have anything to say?"

The class was as quiet as the grave.

"I'm not going to waste the whole afternoon on this," Mr. Delaney finally said. "Danielle, don't worry. We'll find your sweater. We're going to sit here after the final bell until we do." The whole class groaned, but he only looked at us with that no-nonsense expression. "Take out your grammar books," he said. "Now."

I leaned down to get my book out of my knapsack. As I pulled it out, something fuzzy and pink fell out. It was Danielle Larkworthy's sweater! And it was right next to my leaky pen. There was a big blue blob right on the lace collar. With a swift kick, I sent the sweater flying down the aisle. It landed at Katie Riggs's feet.

"Hey!" she said. "It's your sweater, Danielle! Ewww, gross. There's ink all over it." Katie held it up and waved it around. Then she tossed it back to Danielle. Danielle's lower lip started to wobble.

This time, I thought Mr. Delaney was going to explode. He didn't say anything for a minute. He just looked at us, one by one, his lips tight.

"If I see one more example of vandalism in this class, every single person will be in very big trouble. That's trouble with a capital *T*," he said in a clipped, furious tone "Now, open your books to page sixty-seven."

He turned to the blackboard and began copying a sentence from the textbook onto it. I started to open my book, but I noticed that there was an eraser on my desk. Where had that come from? Frowning, I picked it up.

Suddenly, the eraser flew out of my hand. It sailed over every head in the third row and bonked Mr. Delaney in the head. Everyone gasped and looked at me.

Slowly, Mr. Delaney turned. His face was beet-red. "Who...did...that?"

Nobody said anything. That's the thing adults don't realize about kids—we're incredibly loyal to each other. It's us against them.

"If I don't find out, this class will be spending *Saturday* at school," Mr. Delaney said.

"But Saturday's the Winter Festival!" Cissy Oppenheimer said. She looked like she was going to cry again.

"Exactly," Mr. Delaney said. "Now, I'm asking one more time, class. Who threw that eraser?"

"Toby!" everyone in the class shouted.

10

Big Trouble

I'd been in trouble at school before. Once, I'd passed a note to Brian during a boring movie called *Those Amazing Marsupials*. And last year, I'd stuck out my foot as teacher's pet Boyd Wilkins was running to erase the board. I hadn't expected him to crash into Mrs. Patterson!

But I'd never been in trouble like this. This wasn't just trouble. This was Big Trouble. This was calling-your-mother-for-a-conference trouble.

Mom went to the school to see Mr. Delaney after work that very day. I decided it would be an excellent time to do some chores. I started with the breakfast dishes.

Buddy had disappeared for the rest of the "fun-filled" afternoon. Mr. Delaney had yelled at me. Every student in sixth grade had turned against me. And Brian had left early so he wouldn't have to walk home with me.

I was washing the juice glasses when Buddy showed up. Even with my back to the room, I knew that he was there. The kitchen smelled like it had when we'd gone away for two weeks and a raccoon had died on the back porch.

"I know you're there, Buddy," I said, pulling a glass out of the soapy water.

"I know you know, kid."

I turned around and saw him. The glass slipped from my soapy hand and smashed on the floor.

Buddy's skin looked as though it was melting off his bones. His eye sockets were practically hollow, making his face skull-like.

"What's happening to you?" I asked.

"Every time I materialize, I decay a little more," Buddy said. "It's getting worse and worse."

That was really something to look forward to. Buddy was turning into a rotting corpse right in front of my eyes!

"You'd better clean up that glass," Buddy said. "You're in enough trouble as it is."

"Thanks to you," I said, going to the closet for the broom.

"Hey, I had to put some pressure on Gerry,"

Buddy said. "He was sweet on Chi Chi, too."

"Boy," I said. "She sure got around."

"Nah," Buddy said. "Chi Chi didn't go for Gerry's type. But the night of the prom, she was going to get a ride home with him. She and I'd had a fight that night."

"So what did bonking him on the head with an eraser tell you?" I asked.

"I wanted to see if he'd lose his temper," Buddy said. "But that cat was pretty cool."

"I can't see Mr. Delaney murdering anyone," I said.

"You never know," Buddy said with a shrug. "Listen, kid, I'm going upstairs to do some thinking. I've got to come up with our next move."

"Sounds like a terrific idea," I said. As soon as Buddy left, I got out the Lysol and gave the air a good spray. Then, since I had the broom out, I figured it wouldn't hurt to sweep the floor. Just as I was dumping the last bit of dirt into the garbage, Mom walked through the back door.

"I hope you don't think that's going to do you one bit of good," she said, pointing at the broom.

"No," I said. "I'm not that stupid."

Mom stood in the middle of the kitchen floor. She didn't even take off her coat. "What's going on, Toby?" she said. "Bubble bath in the aquarium? Ink on Danielle's sweater? Hitting Gerry—

Mr. Delaney—with an eraser? And he told me you cut school yesterday. That doesn't sound like you."

"I know," I mumbled.

"So what's going on?" Mom repeated.

"Nothing," I said.

"Mr. Delaney is worried about you. So am I. Toby, you have to tell me if something's bothering you. Are you having trouble with someone at school, maybe? Craig Rawley?"

Mom looked really upset. I felt terrible, but what could I do? I couldn't tell her about Buddy. She'd haul me off to a loony bin.

"There's nothing wrong," I said. "I goofed off. But I've been good all my life. So what if I was bad for two days? Big deal."

Mom's brown eyes snapped with anger. "It's a very big deal when you destroy property and lie. In fact, maybe you need some time to think about what a very big deal it is." I'd never seen her so angry. "You're grounded for the rest of the month. I want you to come home straight after school. And Winter Festival is definitely out."

"All right, Mom," I said, beginning to feel cheerful. I couldn't help Buddy now! He'd have to haunt somebody else.

"Don't smirk at me, young man!" Mom

snapped. "I'm going to call here at three-fifteen every day to make sure you're here. And I'll keep calling to make sure you stay!" She yanked off her coat. "Now listen up. Mrs. Andover is off visiting her sister in Boston, so I told her we'd watch Sweetie Pie. That will keep you busy for the next week."

"Okay, Mom," I said, frowning.

"I left her on the front porch, but I don't want her gnawing on the railing," Mom said. "Take her up to your room. I want you to get started on your homework immediately."

"Okay, Mom," I said. I hesitated. Mom seemed so disappointed. "I'm sorry," I said.

She nodded. "An apology is a start. But you need to *show* me that you're sorry by obeying me."

Mom was banging pots and pans when I let Sweetie Pie in from the porch. She butted her big head against my leg, and I petted her.

Sweetie Pie trotted behind me as I grabbed my backpack and headed upstairs. But when we got to my room, she stopped dead and started to whine.

"Come on," I said.

Sweetie Pie backed away, shaking her head.

I crouched down next to her. "I know," I said

in her ear. "There's something weird in there. But he won't hurt you. Don't be scared."

Sweetie Pie still wouldn't move, so I took her by the collar and pulled her inside. I shut the door and she pressed against it.

Buddy appeared, sitting on my desk. "So who's the pooch?"

Sweetie Pie began to growl.

"She belongs to my neighbor," I said. "I have to watch her. And thanks to you, I'm grounded. So you'd better find somebody else to help you."

Buddy laughed. "Forget it, bub. You ain't getting off that easy."

"I won't do it, Buddy!" I said angrily. "I won't lie to Mom again. She trusts me."

"Ooo, you're breaking my heart," Buddy said.

"And I have to watch Sweetie Pie," I said.

"This isn't a kennel, kid," Buddy said.

"I won't do it!" I said, clenching my fist. I was sick of being pushed around by a ghost.

Suddenly my desk lamp went out. In the dusky light, Buddy seemed to glow.

"I won't," I said.

That's when I saw something seeping down the walls of my room. Slowly it trailed down the wallpaper, dark and thick. Was it blood?

Sweetie Pie was whining and scratching at the door to get out. I didn't blame her. Buddy rose off the desk, straight into the air. His eyes were glowing red in their hollowed-out sockets. He raised a bony hand and pointed at the dog.

Then, with a snap of Buddy's fingers, Sweetie Pie disappeared!

11

Sweetie Pie Gets Zapped

The lights came back on and Buddy slowly lowered himself to the desk. The wallpaper had blue and white stripes, like always, and the blood had disappeared. But Sweetie Pie was still gone.

I was shaking all over. "Where's Sweetie Pie?" I asked in a squeaky voice. I looked under my bed, then in the closet.

"Don't bother looking for her, kid," Buddy said.

"But she's my responsibility!" I cried. "And Mrs. Andover *loves* her. You've got to tell me what you did with her!"

"She's in, uh—detention. You know, like another dimension." Buddy shrugged. "It's where I am, too, most of the time. She'll get used to it."

"How can you hurt an innocent dog?"

"She won't be hurt or sad. She won't be happy either. Look, kid. I'm not alive, but I'm not really dead. It's kinda hard to explain if you haven't been there. And you wouldn't want to be there, would you, kid?" Buddy's voice was low and sinister.

"No," I admitted. I was terrified. "But why are you picking on me? I'm not the only person on earth who can fix your problem."

"Not so, kid," Buddy said. "You're in the Shadow Zone, get it?"

"The Shadow Zone?" I said blankly.

Buddy shrugged. "It's another dimension, like I told you. Only a lucky few can enter."

"Yeah, real lucky," I muttered. But I decided not to push the issue. "So I'm trapped in some shadow?"

Buddy nodded. "Think of it like a storm cloud. And the only way you're going to change the weather is by helping me." His sunken gray eyes bored into mine. "Got the picture, kid?"

I nodded slowly.

"Good. Because I had another notion," Buddy said. "Prom night was a gas. It was a big night for the class of '62. Some weird things happened. Besides me croaking, I mean." Buddy held up a skeletal hand and began to tick off items on his bony fingers. "Ray's mother died. She had a heart attack that day and was rushed to the hospital. T. C. Toomer and Elsie Polansky got engaged. Chi Chi broke up with me. Somebody stole my ID bracelet."

"But what does that have to do with your being murdered?" I asked.

"I think whoever stole the ID bracelet killed me," Buddy said. "Because whoever stole it overheard something they shouldn't have."

"What?" I asked. I sat down on the bed. I was starting to get interested in spite of being so scared.

"Chi Chi and I had a fight. The real knockdown-drag-out type. In the hall, outside the gym. I didn't like her hanging out with Elsie and T. C. and that squirt Gerry Delaney. A real bunch of cubes. So I told her that her fancy crowd wasn't as smart as she thought. That one of them bought some answers to the chemistry exam from me."

"You sold answers to an *exam?*" I asked.

Buddy gave a crooked smile. "I never said I was a saint, kid."

"That's for sure," I muttered.

"But my little piece of information backfired. Chi Chi was even madder at me for selling the test. She blew a gasket and threw my ID bracelet at me. I was too cool to pick it up, so I let her storm off and followed her real casual-like, to show I didn't care. But I went back to get it a minute later. I mean, it was my ID, man. But it was gone. That means that whoever took it had been there the whole time. Probably in one of those dark corners in the hall."

"So what are you saying, Buddy?" I asked.

"Maybe if we look at the yearbook pictures we could find out who stole it."

"Why?" I asked, puzzled.

"You see, we had the fight right when the conga line was starting."

"What's a conga line?"

"It's this lame-o dance, don't worry about it. But anyway, the yearbook photographer took a zillion pictures. His girlfriend was at the head of the line. I remember the flash popping in the gym like crazy. So what we gotta do is look at the pictures to see who was missing. We might even see if someone is wearing my ID in a later picture. You dig?"

I nodded. "And then we'd know—"

"Who murdered me," Buddy said matter-of-factly. "I figure it this way. It's either someone who was jealous of me and wanted Chi Chi for himself. Or it's the person who bought the exam questions. I'm betting on that cat myself. He had the most to lose. If he hadn't graduated, he wouldn't have been able to walk into the cushy job his daddy arranged."

I leaned closer. "So who bought the questions?"

"T. C. Toomer," Buddy said.

"*Chief* Toomer? But he's the head of the police department! He stands for law and order. Justice. Liberty."

"So what?"

"He wouldn't murder anybody over a stupid test," I said. "Would he?"

"One thing I've learned from being dead, kid. Life is strange." Buddy sighed. "So tomorrow after school we pay a visit to the Toomer house. No warrant."

"Just a little B and E," I said weakly.

Buddy smiled his chilling, white-gummed smile. "You're learning, kid."

I lucked out the next day. Unbelievable, huh? I figured my luck had flown out the window when Buddy had floated through my doorway.

Mom had to do some Winter Festival stuff with Elsie Toomer that afternoon. She was even getting time off from work. That meant that she wouldn't be at her office to call me every half hour to make sure I was home. And it meant that we knew for sure that Elsie Toomer would be out of the house for an hour or so.

Of course, I *was* about to break into the

house of the chief of police. But at least they didn't have a dog.

The Toomers' house was about eight blocks away, in a better neighborhood than ours. I dropped off my books at home after school and jogged over.

It was a cold day, and no one was around. Keeping close to the bushes on the side of the house, I ran to the backyard. Then I dashed across the patio to the back door.

I still had the pick Buddy had given me, but I didn't need it. I just turned the knob, and the door opened. Elsie Toomer was a little spacey, so I wasn't surprised to find the door unlocked. Or maybe she figured nobody would have the nerve to break into the house of the chief of police.

With that cheery thought, I cautiously pushed the door open and stepped inside.

"How about this, man," Buddy said, materializing next to me. "No B. Just E."

Beyond the kitchen I could see into the dining room. It was full of little china knickknacks and a silver tea set. It was a perfect place for a kid and an obnoxious ghost to get into trouble.

I walked in and inched around the furniture. The adjoining living room contained even more little china statues on rickety little tables.

"Heads up!" Buddy called, and a porcelain shepherdess came flying at me.

"Hey!" I backed up, almost upsetting a table. I reached out, and the shepherdess fell into my sweaty palms. "Buddy!" I yelled, but he only laughed and disappeared.

"What a clown," I muttered. Carefully I placed the china piece back on a shelf and beat it out of the living room. Outside in the front hall, boxes were stacked against the wall.

I heard Buddy's voice float downstairs. "Get a move on, bub."

I followed the voice to a curving staircase. Buddy was floating a few inches off the ground at the top. His face glowed eerily white, and his eye sockets were more sunken than ever. I couldn't believe I was walking *toward* him instead of running away. But there was no escaping a ghost.

"Check the study up here," Buddy said when I reached the top. "I bet the yearbook is in those bookshelves."

Hurrying upstairs, I followed Buddy, who floated into a book-lined study. There were shelves and shelves of books from floor to ceiling.

"It'll take all afternoon!" I wailed.

"Then you'd better start, kiddo. I'm gonna

check out the bedroom." Buddy disappeared.

I sighed and started with the shelves by the window. I just had to be home by four. Mom would probably call as soon as she finished seeing Mrs. Toomer. I drummed my fingers nervously against my leg as I scanned the titles.

There it was! The yearbook for Tilson High, Class of '62. I reached for it just as I heard the sound of the key in the lock downstairs.

Someone was home. But I wasn't as worried this time. The Toomer house was huge, and there was plenty of room to hide.

I drifted back toward the door to listen. I heard Elsie Toomer's high-pitched voice. Had she finished the Winter Festival work early? I'd better get home, pronto. Mom would be calling soon.

"There's just one more box upstairs," Elsie said. "Ooo, I'm so *tired.*"

Then I heard another voice. It was Mom's.

"That's okay, Elsie," she said. "I'll go upstairs and get it."

Nervously, I backed up a few steps. That's when I fell over a big brown box and landed on the floor with a *thump*.

12

Mom's Big Surprise

Frantically, I glanced around. There was a door on the other side of the desk. Clutching my knee, I hopped to the door.

Why did Buddy always disappear at the wrong time? When the going got tough, that ghoul got going. I'd rather be anywhere but here right now—even in another dimension!

I heard Mom climbing the stairs. When I opened the door, I found it was a small bathroom. I shut the door just as she walked into the study.

"I found it, Elsie!" Mom called downstairs. I heard the sound of the box being hefted. "Oof," Mom muttered. "You'd think she'd offer to help."

The box dropped again. "Is it heavy?" Elsie called from downstairs.

"A little," Mom called.

"I wish I could help, Charlene," Elsie said.

"But you know how delicate I am."

"Who am I, Arnold Schwarzenegger?" Mom muttered.

I looked around the bathroom, just in case. There was no shower or bathtub, so there was no shower curtain to hide behind. The small window was too tiny to crawl through. In other words, if Mom decided to use the bathroom, I was sunk.

I backed up, thinking of this, and my hand hit the plastic cup on the edge of the sink. It fell into the sink with a clatter. Yikes!

I heard Mom hesitate. "Is someone in there? T. C.?"

I held my breath.

"Elsie?" she shouted. "Is someone home?"

"Nobody here but us chickens, Charlene!" Elsie called merrily.

I heard Mom take a step toward the bathroom. I looked around wildly. There had to be some way out! Maybe I could wrap myself in towels and pretend to be a sheikh.

As I heard Mom tentatively tiptoeing toward the door, I noticed something. There was a built-in hamper in the wall. I opened it and saw that it was one of those old-fashioned kinds. The clothes went down a long chute. It probably

went down to the laundry room in the basement. But did the Toomers still use it? Was the
chute still working?

There was a short tap on the door. "Uh—ex-
cuse me. T. C.? Are you in there?"

I balanced on the toilet and put one leg in the
chute, then the other.

The doorknob rattled. "Hello?"

I let go. Down, down, I went into blackness.
It was the longest, scariest ride I'd ever had. Ten
times worse than Chicken Liver Hill. The air
was dark and stuffy, and I was afraid I'd suffo-
cate before I'd get to the end. But then I picked
up speed. I saw a light approaching, and in another second I flew out of the chute and landed
on a pile of the Toomers' dirty laundry.

It was not exactly my idea of fun to land on
Chief Toomer's boxer shorts. But anything was
better than facing Mom. I had to get out of
there!

I rolled off the pile and looked around. There
was a basement window right over the washing
machine. I climbed up and turned the latch to
open it. Then I wiggled through it out into the
cold winter air.

There was no sign of Buddy. No smell, either.
Keeping to the bushes in case Mom looked out
the window, I made a dash for the yard next to

the Toomers'. Then I cut across it to the back fence, climbed over, ran across another yard, and ended up on Woodhill Lane.

It took only ten minutes of a fast jog to make it home. I banged inside, gasping for breath. I looked at the answering machine, but the red light wasn't blinking. Mom hadn't called. I'd made it!

The phone rang, and I took a couple of deep breaths before I picked it up.

"Toby? Why are you out of breath?"

"I, um, was throwing the ball for Sweetie Pie," I said.

"I hope it wasn't in the house," Mom said.

"I was in the back. I heard the phone and ran to get it. I figured it was you."

"Mmmm. Well, I'm still at Mrs. Toomer's. We're going to drop some things at the gym, and then I have to take care of some things at the office. I'll be home around five-thirty."

"Okay, Mom."

"I want you to wash the lettuce for salad and set the table."

"Okay, Mom. I'll be glad to," I said in a cheerful voice.

She laughed a little. "You should get in big trouble more often," she said teasingly. "You seem to enjoy chores so much more."

"Mrs. Bemus didn't raise a dummy," I said.

"Speaking of dummies," Mom said in the same amused voice, "do your homework." Then she said good-bye and hung up. It was nice to have my old mom back. She might be older than most moms, but she was a lot more fun.

Wait a second. *Older than most moms.* Of course! I wasn't sure what year Mom graduated from high school, but she might have a copy of the 1962 yearbook. With luck, I wouldn't have to break into any more houses to find it!

I raced upstairs to her room. Mom kept a couple of boxes of "mementos" in the closet. One box, I knew, held leftover stuff from my dad. Just in case I might want his old Timex watch one day or something. And the other box was full of stuff from before that. I'd never seen her open it.

I peeled back the masking tape and opened the box. I laughed when a hot-pink stuffed poodle looked out at me. It looked like something she'd won at a carnival. There was a little box with a charm bracelet in it. A pair of saddle shoes. Some 45 records. And a pair of turquoise pants with gold fringe running down the leg. I guess they were hot stuff back in the Stone Age.

And then I saw it. *Tilson High, Class of '62.*

I opened the book to the senior-class pictures. I just had to see Buddy. I wanted to see what he looked like when he was alive. I flipped to the Ps and found him, Bernard "Buddy" Parker. The hair was definitely weird, but I had to admit that Buddy had looked kind of handsome before he looked kind of dead.

I flipped back to the Ds and found Gerald "Gerry" Delaney. I laughed out loud. Balding Mr. Delaney had had lots of curly hair. He looked kind of nervous and nerdy, though. "Class Brain" was written under his picture.

I flipped a few pages ahead again to the Fs. My mother's maiden name was Forester. I ran my finger along the names. And there she was— Charlene Forester. Charlene "Chi Chi" Forester!

Chi Chi was my very own mother.

13

Chi Chi's Secret

Mom—a *Chi Chi?*

I stared at the picture. I recognized Mom's smile and her big dark eyes, even with that thick black eyeliner around them. Her hair was a much lighter blond. It was teased and sprayed so it sat on her head like a football helmet.

All the other girls wore pearls around their necks and round-collared white blouses. Mom was wearing a black leotard. Her smile was a little crooked, as though she thought getting her yearbook picture taken was totally square.

Mom was a *Chi Chi!*

Underneath the photos were dumb slogans like "Future Man on the Moon" or "Best Class Secretary Ever!" or "Two-Time Winner of the English Medal." Then there were lists of clubs the student had belonged to, like the Physics Club or the Future Nurses of America.

Under Mom's name was Art Club, Poets'

Society, and: "Founding and Only Member of the Buddy Parker Fan Club."

I carefully closed the box back up. Then I took the yearbook back to my room. I lay on my bed and flipped through the prom pictures. I found the conga line. But I couldn't tell who was missing, if anybody was.

I slid the yearbook in between my mattress and box spring. For some reason, I didn't want Buddy to know I'd found it. Did he know my mother was Chi Chi? I frowned, thinking. He'd never actually been around when Mom was. He usually stayed in my room. And that day on Main Street he'd asked who my mother was. So he didn't know.

Did I really want to tell him? What if he started haunting *Mom?* He'd probably never leave!

I must have fallen asleep, because the next thing I knew I heard Mom calling me downstairs. I had forgotten to wash the lettuce for dinner. I climbed tiredly out of bed and went downstairs.

"I'm sorry," I said when I got to the kitchen. Mom was pulling things out of the fridge for supper. "I fell asleep. I'm really sorry."

She looked over at me. To my relief, she

smiled softly. "It's okay, sleepyhead. Why don't you do it for me now, though? I'm going to make the chicken. Is Sweetie Pie okay?"

"She's sleeping." *Sort of.*

I filled the sink with water and dumped the lettuce in it. Then I attacked the leaves with the sprayer and twirled them in the salad spinner to dry. Mom was a fanatic about her salads.

"Toby, would you cut up a green pepper for me?" Mom asked. She was sautéing chicken in a big pan. I smelled garlic and onions.

I started to slice the green pepper. "Mom, did you know a guy named Buddy Parker?" I asked.

Mom dropped the spatula in the hot oil. It splattered, and she jumped away. "Ow!" She rushed to the sink and stuck her wrist under cold water.

"Are you okay?"

She bit her lip. "Fine. It just splashed me a little, that's all." She went back to the stove and adjusted the heat under the pan. Then she picked up the spatula again. "Why do you ask?" she said in a normal voice.

"Some kids were talking about him at school. They say he smashed into the tree on Chicken Liver Hill. They even say he still haunts it."

"That's ridiculous," Mom said.

"Do you believe in ghosts?" I asked, sneaking

a look at her. But she kept her face away.

"Of course not."

"What about Buddy, Mom? Did you know him?"

"I knew him." She covered the pan and turned away from the stove. "He was...a good friend."

"Was he your boyfriend?"

She gave me a look, as though she wasn't sure I should be asking the question. But then she nodded. "Yes. He was my boyfriend."

"Were you sad when he died?" I asked.

Mom didn't seem to know I was in the room anymore. "I was very sad," she said.

"Did you wonder why he crashed into that tree?" I asked. "Because—"

"Toby, why are you asking me all these questions?" Mom asked sharply. She turned around and started to reslice the green pepper I'd already cut up. "It happened a very long time ago."

"I was just interested, that's all. I was wondering if you ever thought about him."

Mom didn't say anything for several minutes. She wiped off the counter. She checked the potatoes in the oven. She got out the sour cream. She even cut up some chives to go on top of the potatoes.

When she spoke, her voice sounded tight, as though she were squeezing it out of her throat. She sliced the green pepper again. By now, the poor pepper was pulverized.

"I said I didn't believe in ghosts. And I don't. But Buddy's death...haunts me."

"Haunts you?" I asked. A chill walked slowly down my spine. "Why?"

Mom stared at the glistening blade of the kitchen knife. "Because I'm the reason he's dead."

That's all Mom would say. She said she didn't want to talk about it. She said she shouldn't have said what she did. She said everything was fine, and why didn't I go up to my room before dinner?

I was worried...and scared. Was Chi Chi, my mother, the reason Buddy had died? What had Mom meant, anyway? Was she so mad at Buddy that night that she'd tampered with his brakes? Mom knew a car engine inside out. Maybe she didn't mean for him to die. Maybe she just wanted to scare him.

I shook my head to drive away such a stupid thought. Mom wasn't the type to play tricks, or get revenge on people.

But I knew Charlene Bemus. What I didn't

know was what Chi Chi Forester would have done. What would Buddy do if he found out that his beloved Chi Chi had somehow caused his death?

I stopped outside my room. I knew Buddy was inside. I could sense him in there, waiting. I could *smell* him in there, waiting. And I knew he'd stop at nothing to get revenge.

14

High School Horror

I didn't sleep too great that night. *You* try snoozing with a stinking, snoring corpse under your bed.

I tortured myself imagining what Buddy would do to Mom if he knew it was her fault he was dead. Send her to the Shadow Zone? Hang her from the roof? Haunt her with blood dripping down her walls and "Don't Be Cruel" playing on the stereo?

School wasn't any better. Brian was giving me the cold shoulder. He wouldn't talk to me, even after I offered him half of my tuna fish sandwich and my whole bag of potato chips.

Nobody talked to me in the schoolyard. Everybody was still mad at me for trashing the classroom and almost getting the whole class detention.

Across the schoolyard, I could see Craig Rawley whispering with Jeff and Marty. He was probably plotting against me. Brian snuck some looks at me from where he was playing handball with Tony Holland. But he never came over.

I was glad when the last bell rang. I saw Brian kind of lingering near the front door. He was pretending to fiddle with the strap on his backpack, but I knew it was an act. He was waiting for me! He was ready to make up.

I was hurrying toward him when I felt a cold draft. Then an awful smell introduced itself to my nostrils.

The door to the utility closet was cracked. I peeked inside. Buddy was leaning against the wall. He raised a lazy hand and grabbed hold of my collar. He pulled me inside the closet.

"Greetings. Ready to go to work, bub?"

"No."

"Good. We're going to the high school to check out the library. They've gotta have a copy of the '62 yearbook there. Not only that," Buddy said, "they put out this alumni guide that they update all the time."

"Why do you want to see that?" I asked warily.

"Because the time has come," Buddy said. "I'm ready to find Chi Chi."

I was getting so used to B and E that the idea

barely fazed me. Anyway, I was too busy worrying about what would happen when Buddy discovered that Chi Chi was now Mrs. Bemus.

The door to the high school was still open. I pushed inside cautiously. The halls were empty and quiet. I tried to look like an undergrown freshman Chess Club nerd.

"Down this hall, make a right," Buddy said in my ear.

I went down the hall and made a right. "Up the stairs," Buddy said. "The library is right at the top across the hall. This place hasn't changed a bit."

I ran up the stairs. It felt weird to be in Tilson High. In a couple of years I'd be a few inches taller—hopefully—and climbing these stairs every day. That is, if I survived sixth grade.

The library door was locked. I heard footsteps coming up the stairs behind me. "Don't disappear, Buddy," I said in a low voice. "Get me inside this door, now!"

Buddy's voice came from behind the door. "Turn the handle to the left. Wiggle it and push the door at the same time."

The door opened as if by magic. I slipped inside and it closed behind me. Buddy appeared with his ghoulish grin.

"How did you do that?" I gasped.

"Trick lock," Buddy said. "I guess they never fixed it. I used to meet Chi Chi here."

"Oh," I said. "We'd better find the yearbooks, fast."

Buddy drifted off to one corner. "Who's this Dickens guy?" he asked. "I think I heard of him."

"Maybe you *met* him," I mumbled. I scanned the bookshelves anxiously. Buddy disappeared between the bookcases.

I found the yearbooks lined up near the check-out desk. The alumni guide was at the very end, and I slipped it out quickly. My fingers were shaking as I shoved it behind a huge dictionary on the next shelf.

"Hey, Buddy!" I called. "I found the yearbook!" I placed the book on the check-out desk.

Buddy appeared at my elbow. The pages started to flip all by themselves. They stopped briefly at Buddy's senior picture. "What a handsome guy," he said. Then the pages turned until the prom pictures appeared. "What a night," Buddy murmured.

"Do you see anything?" I asked nervously.

Buddy didn't answer. He stared at the pages for a long time. He put his finger on a picture I'd missed. It was of Mom in her prom dress dancing with Gerry Delaney. "Chi Chi must have danced with him after I left," he murmured.

"We'd better go," I said.

"What about the alumni guide?" Buddy asked.

"I can't find it," I said. "They probably don't put one out anymore. School budgets are really strained these days. Computers are expensive."

"Computers?" Buddy asked, puzzled.

I heard footsteps outside the door. Some girl laughed. "Come *on*, Buddy," I urged.

I started out of the library, and Buddy didn't hold me back. I peeked into the hall. Some cheerleaders were just disappearing around the corner. I hurried down the stairs and through the front hall. But when I got to the front door, it was locked.

"Oh, no!" I breathed. Was it as easy to break *out* of a building as it was to break *in*?

"They lock it at four," Buddy said. "I forgot. But no sweat—we can go out through the gym. Follow me."

So I followed a ghost through the halls of Tilson High. We went down a flight of back stairs and arrived outside the gym. I heard voices, and Buddy stopped.

I peeked inside the gym. Elsie Toomer and some other ladies were unpacking boxes. I forgot that they were storing stuff for the rummage sale in the gym.

One of the ladies, Mrs. Fenton, held up a big

pleated skirt with a poodle on it. "Remember these, girls?" she asked.

The other ladies laughed. "Remember our prom?" Mrs. Restivo said. "I went with Gerry Delaney. But he only had eyes for Chi Chi. I guess I should say Charlene now. Buddy was so jealous!"

"Come on, Buddy. Let's go," I said nervously.

"Not yet," Buddy said.

"Poor Chi Chi," Mrs. Fenton said. "Buddy's death just devastated her."

Buddy sighed.

"Come on," I whispered.

Elsie Toomer was folding a tablecloth with an angry gesture. She sniffed. "Devastated? Of course she was. Let's admit it, girls." She leaned forward, her eyes glittering. "We all know the truth. She killed him!"

15

Welcome to My Nightmare

Mom had killed Buddy? I didn't want to believe it. Just then, a chair scraped in the athletic director's office next to us.

"We've got to get out of here!" I hissed. I hurried over to the side door and pushed it open. I was outside and safe.

But how safe was Mom?

Buddy leaned against the school building. His face looked even grayer than usual. His chilling gaze rested on me.

"Don't listen to that Elsie Toomer," I said. "She has the biggest mouth in town. She's always making up stories about people."

"I know, Elsie was like that in high school, too," Buddy said. But his voice sounded funny. Distant. As if he was really thinking of something else. As if he was putting the pieces together. As if he was wondering if Chi Chi had been mad enough to kill him.

All during school the next day, I thought about my problem. I knew it was too big for me to handle all by myself.

That's when I decided. I had to tell Brian about Buddy. Brian was my best friend. I was in trouble. If Brian were me, I'd want me to help him. Or him to help him. Help me. Whatever.

When the last bell rang, I hurried to get my books together. I decided to catch Brian right as he was leaving school.

I was winding my scarf around my neck outside the classroom when somebody pulled it tight from behind. I staggered back a few steps. Buddy!

But then I heard the familiar honk of Craig Rawley's stupid laugh.

"Not so fast, Chicken Liver," he said.

I yanked my scarf back and turned around. Craig, Jeff, and Marty were surrounded by a bunch of boys from the sixth grade. Even Brian was there, looking nervous.

"We're going to have a special contest and we want you in on it, Tobe-er-roni," Craig said, squinting his mean little pig eyes.

"That's okay," I said. "Count me out."

"It's at the Winter Festival," Craig said.

"Too bad," I said. "I'm grounded. I can't go to the Winter Festival this year."

"Oooo, he's *grounded*," Craig said mockingly. "And he's too scared to sneak out! Scared his mommy will punish him!"

"Don't worry, Bemus," Jeff Fingerhut said. "You can wear your knee-pads." Craig and a few of the weenier guys laughed.

"We're going to have a secret Chicken Liver Challenge on the hill," Craig said. "Whoever loses will be the Biggest Chicken Liver of All Time. The prize is a bucket of chicken bones from the Poultry Shack." Craig looked around the group, seeming really pleased with himself. "Who's with me?"

I started to fade back. There was no way I was going to get involved. I had enough to worry about!

Craig turned around, slowly eyeing the kids. "C'mon. Or are you a bunch of *Chicken Livers* like Baby Bemus?" he sneered.

One by one, the guys raised their hands. Even some of the girls did. That made even *more* boys raise their hands. Everybody did except Brian and Chester Van Owen. Both of them were too smart to give in to Craig Rawley.

I was already at the edge of the circle. I was about to cut away and fade back to the door when invisible hands grabbed my elbows. I was pushed forward into the crowd, right up front. I felt my arm yanked, and it waved, right in front of Craig Rawley's face!

"Hey, looks like Chicken Liver Bemus is ready to humiliate himself once again," Craig hooted.

"And this time it'll be in front of the whole class!" Marty Lazar jeered. Jeff Fingerhut made chicken noises.

Great. Now Buddy had *really* done it. I had to brave Chicken Liver Hill in front of the entire sixth-grade class!

Everybody slowly straggled away. I knew Buddy had left, too. He usually disappeared for a couple of hours after he'd done something mean. Brian trudged off toward the school door, his bright orange backpack clashing with his green coat.

"Brian, wait up!" I hurried after him.

He waited, but he didn't look happy about it. "Why'd you do that, Toby?" he said. "You always let Craig get to you. He's just a big bully."

"I know," I said. "But—"

"You always let people dare you into doing stupid things so they won't think you're a nerd." Brian's face was pale and serious.

"Face it, Toby," he said. "You *are* a nerd. So am I. School is tough for guys like us. But at least we're smart. Someday we'll be lawyers or writers or senators while Craig Rawley is pumping gas and waiting all week for *Monday Night Football*. He'll end up sad and lonesome like Ray Ebsen."

Hearing Ray Ebsen's name reminded me of why I'd stopped Brian. "The thing is," I said, "I *didn't* volunteer for the Chicken Liver Challenge."

"What do you mean? I saw you," Brian said.

"Somebody pushed me," I said. "And somebody raised my hand for me."

"Oh, come on," Brian said. "I didn't see anybody."

"That's just it!" I said excitedly. "You didn't *see* anybody. Look, I know this is going to sound super weird. But it was a ghost, Brian. The ghost of Chicken Liver Hill. His name is Buddy. He's been haunting me. You see—"

But Brian was backing up, shaking his head. He didn't look scared, or nervous. He looked mad. "You're a loser, Toby Bemus," he said furiously. "A real jerk. You don't have to bother making up a bunch of lies. If you don't want to be my friend anymore, just say so!"

"Brian, listen to me," I said. "I'm telling you the truth!"

"The truth? That a ghost named *Buddy* is haunting you?" Brian scoffed. "Come on! What is it? Do you have a new best friend? Or do you have a girlfriend?"

No, I wanted to say. I have a *ghoul* friend. But Brian was too mad.

"Brian, I need help," I pleaded. "I really am being haunted. By a ghost."

Brian just stared at me. "Forget it. I'm out of here," he said. Then he walked away.

There was a freezing rainstorm that night. Hail rattled against the windows. It took me a while to fall asleep.

It was dark when I woke up, and the rain had stopped. I felt myself being lifted, but I couldn't see who was doing it. I tried to ask what was going on, but I was so sleepy I couldn't talk. Then I felt myself being lowered again. But it didn't feel like I was put back in bed. Something creaked, then clicked, and the darkness seemed even blacker.

I reached out my arms to my sides and touched something soft. My fingers ran over it and found that I was surrounded by soft satin. I reached up and felt wood over my head.

And then terror struck. *I was in a coffin!*

I banged my fists against the top. I screamed. But the wood was thick, and I knew my voice wouldn't carry. I screamed and screamed. I pounded as hard as I could. I was buried alive!

Tap. Tap. Tap. Someone was signaling me on the top of the coffin. It must be Mom! She knew I wasn't dead!

"Mom? Mom!" I shouted.

"Yes, dear. Toby, wake up!"

I opened my eyes. It was morning. Mom was standing in the doorway holding a pile of clean laundry. It must have been her tapping on the door that woke me up. She came over and sat down on my bed. "Did you have a bad dream, sweetie?"

I bolted upright. "Mom! What are you doing here!" I flopped over to look under the bed. No Buddy.

"I'm bringing you some fresh laundry, silly," Mom said. "Are you sure you're okay?"

I nodded. My head still felt fuzzy. The nightmare had felt so *real.*

Mom smoothed the blanket. "I wanted to talk to you before I left to set up for the Winter Festival. I've been thinking it over, Toby. I've been too harsh. You've looked forward to the festival for months. I want you to go today."

"That's okay, Mom," I said. "I don't have to." I didn't *want* to. If I went, Buddy went with me. And he'd see Chi Chi—I mean, Mom.

"But I *want* you to," Mom said. "I know you're

100

sorry about the trouble you caused. You haven't been yourself, I can see that. I want you to have fun today with your friends."

What friends? "Really, Mom," I said, "I should stay home. It's only right."

Mom frowned. "I want you to have fun today, young man. And that's final. Now come downstairs. I made oatmeal."

"Okay," I mumbled.

She put the pile of laundry on my desk. "Where's Sweetie Pie?" she asked.

"I guess she went downstairs," I said. "I'll find her."

"Okay. Hurry up, though."

I looked under the bed again. No Buddy. That was weird. But at least I didn't have to worry about his seeing Mom. I'd have to come up with a plan to keep them apart today.

I thought about it as I ate my oatmeal. Mom came into the kitchen wearing her coat and scarf. She was carrying a box of cupcakes she'd baked for the bake sale, as well as a shopping bag full of junk she was donating to the church rummage sale.

"I have to run now, Toby. I'll see you at the festival. Stop by the bake sale booth." Mom kissed me on the top of my head on her way out.

I finished my oatmeal, and just as I put my bowl in the sink, Mom stomped back in. She looked exasperated.

"That darn car!" she exploded. "I just tuned and timed it a month ago. But it's so finicky on cold days. I'm going to have to call a cab."

I left her muttering and dialing the only cab company in town. Then I went back upstairs to make sure Buddy was out of sight. He was. I couldn't find him anywhere. It was definitely weird.

A few minutes later, I heard a horn honk. Mom called upstairs. "I'm leaving, hon!"

"Bye!" I called, then looked outside my bedroom window.

Mom was struggling down the snowy walk with her packages. The cabdriver didn't even get out to help. He just stared straight ahead, a cap pulled over his eyes. Mom pushed her packages into the backseat and then slid inside.

The car engine revved. The driver turned and looked straight up at my window. When he saw me, he smiled.

Even across the distance, I could see the glittering gray eyes. It was Buddy! And he had Mom!

16

Tricks and Bones

I pounded on the glass and screamed, but Mom didn't look up. The cab pulled away and disappeared around the corner. I watched my mother being driven away by a ghoul. Where was he taking her? Would I ever see her again?

I sprang into action, pulling on clothes and my jacket and scarf. I even remembered my gloves. I would start at the church parking lot. If Mom wasn't there setting up, I'd comb the entire town. Then—I didn't know what I'd do. But I'd do something. I'd take Buddy by his bony neck and *make* him tell me what he'd done with Mom.

It was too icy to ride my bike, so I had to run all the way. I was huffing and puffing as I got to Ash Lane, which led into Main Street. I had to slow down. As I walked, I prayed. *Please let her be there. Please let her be there.*

I rounded the corner. The church parking lot

was about four blocks down Main Street. I lunged ahead, looking for my mom's bright-red jacket.

And then I saw her. She was unloading bakery boxes from the back of Bubba Parisi's van. I ran up to her. "Mom! Are you okay?"

"I'm fine." Mom looked amused. "Why wouldn't I be?"

"Uh, was the cab ride okay?"

She nodded. "Sure. Why wouldn't it be?"

Suddenly I was embarrassed. "Uh, I don't know. I'll see you later."

"Have a cranberry muffin," she said, stuffing one in my pocket.

I walked off. Why had Buddy scared me like that? Had he *planned* to do something to Mom and then changed his mind? Was it a warning?

I walked behind the church into the small cemetery that had been there since the 1700s. Someone was sitting with his back to me on a small iron bench. It was awfully cold to be sitting still like that. Your blood would probably freeze. No human could...uh-oh.

I walked closer. "Hi, Buddy."

He looked up, and he looked awful. His skin was gray and hung in pouches off his bones. His eyes looked like a dead flounder's.

"I know that you've been keeping something from me, kid."

"Hey, I just found out," I said. "And why'd you drive her to town? You scared me to death." I eyed him. "You probably scared *her* to death."

"She didn't see me. She saw what she *wanted* to see." Buddy looked away. "Just a cabdriver. She did say I seemed familiar, though."

"Buddy," I blurted, "you don't really think Mom killed you, do you?"

"She was mad at me that night," Buddy said slowly. "And Chi Chi knew her way around an engine. Maybe she's the one who cut the brake line in my car."

"Impossible!" I protested, even though I knew it could be true.

"So who'd she marry?" Buddy asked softly. "Who was your dad?"

"Nathan Bemus," I said. "He was older than Mom. He owned the hardware store in town."

"Nathan Bemus!" Buddy shook his head. "What a drip! I can't believe Chi Chi went for such a square. What happened?"

"He ran away with a waitress from the diner," I said. "It was his forty-fifth birthday. My mom had this surprise party all planned. He never showed up. He took out all their savings and bought a red convertible and drove to California."

"You see? What a drip. Serves her right for forgetting me," Buddy said darkly.

"She didn't marry my dad until years after you were gone," I pointed out. "Was she supposed to lock herself in a closet and bawl about it forever?"

"Naw," Buddy said. "But it woulda saved a lot of tears if I wasn't killed in the first place."

"Buddy, you don't believe that my mom—Chi Chi—"

His eyes were cold. "We'll find out today," he said. "I've got a few tricks up my sleeve." He pushed up his sleeve. There was only a bone where his arm should be. He gave a blood-curdling laugh. "Ready, set, go," he whispered.

Pretty soon, I saw what "tricks" Buddy had in mind. By noon, the parking lot had filled up. It seemed like everyone in town was there.

The first thing happened when Chief Toomer arrived. He strutted around in his police uniform, saying a word here and there to everybody, as though he were running the show. Finally he stood by the muffin table, scarfing free muffins off Mom.

And then, at his feet, an unseen hand started to write letters in the snow.

C-H-E...Chief Toomer snitched another cranberry muffin. He munched happily. A-T-E...

He accepted a cup of steaming coffee.

Chief Toomer looked down just as the R was completed. I saw him jump. His lips moved as they formed the letters.

Cheater!

Chief Toomer coughed. Coffee spewed out of his mouth and hit the snow, dissolving the word. He coughed again and looked around, scared and guilty.

Over in the lot, I saw Ray Ebsen's van pull up and park. As I watched, the letters were forming in the fog on his windshield. T-H-I-E-F.

Thief!

Ray looked at the letters. His face flushed. Then he wiped them off with his sleeve.

I moved over to the pies. Elsie Toomer was decorating the pumpkin spice pies with whipped cream from a can. She put the can down and turned away to cut a slice of apple pie for someone.

The can lifted into the air. On a nice, fresh pie, I watched the letters form in little puffs of cream. L-I-A-R.

Liar!

Elsie turned back, saw the pie, and screamed.

Mom looked up from where she was decorating cupcakes with M & Ms. She dropped the half-full bag on the table and hurried away to help Elsie. I saw the bag tip over and spill out. Slowly, so that nobody noticed, the M & Ms made a heart. Then the letters slowly spelled out *Gerry loves Chi Chi!*

Mr. Delaney was sitting at the next table selling raffle tickets. I saw him look over. He blushed as he read the words and tore off a whole fistful of tickets for a surprised kid.

Mom hurried back to the cupcake table. She saw the heart and looked over at Mr. Delaney. Her face was as red as his.

Quickly, I ducked behind a tree. Craig Rawley saw me and came over. "Trying to hide out?"

"Huh?"

"Forget it, Bemus. It's time for the Chicken Liver Challenge. Everyone's already on the hill."

"I—uh, forgot my sled," I told him.

"No problem!" He punched me on the arm. "We'll get you a loaner!"

I trudged up the hill behind Craig. When we got to the top, Jeff Fingerhut was already on his sled, waiting to go. Brian stood beside Danielle and her friends. I stayed on the other side of the hill, away from everyone else. I stood in the shadows of a pine tree and watched.

Jeff took off. It was clear from the start that the icy rain last night had made the hill faster than ever. Jeff must have been nervous, because when his hat blew off he reached for it with both hands and tumbled off the sled. The sled flew down the hill and crashed into the elm.

It was like that all day. Everyone was too scared of the speed of the slope to make it much past Jellyfish. Craig made it to the Ninja border and rolled off fast. But after Greg Callan lost control and plowed into the old fence and got a bloody nose, kids started rolling off as soon as they got to the Jellyfish border.

"Oh, boy," I groaned. I just knew I'd be the Biggest Chicken Liver of All Time. The pile of bones was waiting for me.

Speaking of a pile of bones, Buddy appeared in the shadows.

"Scared?"

"You bet."

"I'll handle it," Buddy said. "Trust me."

"Trust *you*?" I practically shouted.

"So what *is* a Terminator, anyway?" Buddy asked.

"Toby-Wan Kenobi!" Craig called from across the hill. "You're up!"

I got on the sled. I squinted down the hill. I saw the icy paths of runners down the slope. I saw the crazy track where Greg had lost control. I even saw the blood on the snow from his nose.

I felt a weight settle on top of me. "Buddy?" I muttered.

"You gotta have a little trust, kid," he said, right in my ear. "Let's go."

Somebody—probably Craig—gave us a push. In another moment, we were rocketing down the hill. I've never gone so fast on a sled in my life. The icy wind blew against my face, making my eyes tear. No wonder so many kids couldn't make it far.

Whoosh! We were past Jellyfish. I could hear kids screaming at the top of the hill as I maneuvered the sled to avoid the fence.

Whoosh! We were into Ninja territory! I had passed Craig!

Screams and shouts came from the top of the hill. I got ready to roll off.

But I couldn't! Buddy was on top of me. His weight was pinning me down. I couldn't move! I was going farther than even the eighth-grade boys.

"Buddy!" I panted. "Get off! We're almost to Terminator! We're going to hit the tree!"

"Trust me." The words froze my ear in more ways than one.

Because suddenly, we were zooming past the Terminator mark and heading straight for the tree!

17

Terminator!

"Buddy!" I screamed.

But he didn't answer.

The tree trunk loomed in front of me. There was no room to turn away. We were going to hit!

Suddenly the sled started to tilt. I tightened my grip as it raised up on one runner. Sparks flew as the sled cleared the space with a fraction of an inch to spare.

I heard cheers and screams from the hill, but I didn't have time to really register them. We were going so fast now that we were actually airborne. We flew for a stretch, bumped down, and zoomed down the rest of the trail.

We cleared the trees at the end of the parking lot and slid out into the lot. The sled picked up speed over a patch of ice. We were heading straight for the rummage sale table! People turned and saw me and scattered, muffins and cookies and cups of coffee flying.

Sparks flew from my runners as they hit concrete. I plowed straight into the table. It turned over and all the items went flying.

I rolled off the sled and shook my head dizzily. A small blue-enameled box was spiraling downward through the air. It landed in my lap.

Elsie Toomer pushed through the crowd. "Don't you touch that, Toby Bemus!" she screeched. "That's mine!"

I was still dizzy, so I shook my head again.

"It *is!* And I didn't donate it!" she said angrily. "What's it doing in the rummage sale?" She glared at her husband. "Did you donate it?"

"I've never even *seen* it before," the chief said.

Mom bent over me. "Are you all right?"

I nodded, and her relief turned to anger "Where did you come from? The hill? Don't tell me that you went down that hill on a *sled!*"

Before I could answer, Elsie tapped my mother on the shoulder. "You did it, Charlene! You took the box when you came over the other day!"

Mom looked puzzled. "Why would I do that?"

Elsie bit her lip. "Because...because...it's my special memento box and I want it back! Give it to me, young man!"

She reached over and tried to snatch it out of

my hand. I tried to let go, but something pressed my fingers on the box. Buddy!

Elsie's face got red. "Let go!" she said. She pulled hard, and the box flew out of my hand and popped up. It landed on the concrete, bursting open and spilling out its contents.

A pressed rose. A tube of Brylcreem. A half-smoked cigarette. And an ID bracelet.

The name on the bracelet winked up at us in the sunshine. BUDDY.

"It's Buddy's ID bracelet!" I exclaimed.

"It is," Mom said slowly. She looked up. "How did you get it, Elsie?"

'Yes, Elsie," Chief Toomer said. "How *did* you get it?"

"Buddy gave it to me," Elsie said defiantly. But when everyone just kept staring at her, something seemed to collapse in her face. "Not really," she said faintly. "Charlene threw it at him, and I picked it up. I wanted it!" she said in a sudden fierce voice. "I loved him!"

She leaned over to pick up the other items. She put the pressed rose into the box. "He left this for you on your desk one morning. I took it. I took whatever he touched." She looked up at Mom. "And you killed him! I heard the terrible things you said to him. You didn't love him. You got him so upset he drove into that tree!"

Mr. Delaney moved forward. "That's enough, Elsie," he said in a firm voice. "Buddy's death wasn't Charlene's fault. It was an accident."

"It *was* my fault," Mom suddenly said. "I threw his ID at him." She turned to Mr. Delaney. "I said I was going home with you. I told Buddy he'd never make anything of himself. I told him he didn't have a future."

"No, Chi Chi," Buddy said. "I loved you."

Mom looked up. She put a hand on her heart and looked all around. "What did you say?" she whispered to me in a shaky voice.

"Nothing," I said. Buddy was here, listening to every word. Mom looked confused. But she didn't look scared.

"Buddy Parker committed suicide," Chief Toomer snapped. "He always was a loser."

Ray Ebsen stepped forward. "Speaking of losers, T. C., how did you do on that chemistry test senior year?"

I heard Buddy's soft laugh. Mom jumped, startled.

"Who remembers?" Chief Toomer said, shrugging.

"You shouldn't have graduated, but you did," Ray said. "Thanks to Buddy."

The chief stepped toward Ray. "So you're the one who wrote that in the snow," he growled.

Ray looked surprised. "Wrote what?"

"You know what," Chief Toomer said.

"Why is everyone arguing?" Elsie said in a too-bright voice. "Let's get back to the festival activities."

"That's right," the chief agreed. "Enough of Buddy Parker. He drove that car into a tree by himself. End of story."

"Not quite," Ray said. "Buddy didn't *drive* into that tree, and I've got proof."

That got everyone's attention.

"In shop class that day we were working on brakes," Ray said. "We needed a car to work on. Buddy had cut class, as usual. So I volunteered his car. I guess someone did a bad job on the brakes."

"Maybe somebody did a bad job on purpose," Elsie Toomer said. She looked at Ray. "Someone who wanted to steal Chi Chi."

"Now hold on a minute," Ray said nervously. Chief Toomer put his hand on his holster.

"Just wait a second, everyone," Mr. Delaney said quietly. "I remember that day. Ray had to leave in the middle of class because his mother was rushed to the hospital. Remember, Ray?"

Ray nodded. "I'll never forget that day."

"And then we had a fire drill," Mr. Delaney said. "By the time we got back to class, there wasn't any more time." He looked around at everyone. "Don't you see? *We never finished the job.* Buddy didn't have any brakes that night!"

"And he didn't know it," Mom said. "We rode to the prom with Elsie and T. C., so when he got in his car, he thought it was fine."

"It was nobody's fault," Mr. Delaney said. "Buddy shouldn't have taken his car out of the shop garage at all. It was just a stupid accident."

"So it wasn't my fault," Mom murmured.

"Nobody ever thought it was, Charlene," Mr. Delaney said. He put his hand on her shoulder.

"Nobody," Buddy said.

Mom whipped her head around and looked at me. "Why did you ask me if I believed in ghosts?" she whispered.

"No reason," I said.

She nodded slowly. For a minute she looked kind of dreamy. Then she told me, "Don't go down that hill again on a sled."

"I won't," I said. "Believe me, I won't."

18

Bye-Bye, Buddy

Now that the truth was out, all the adults started to apologize to each other. Elsie Toomer started to cry and hug Mom. Chief Toomer shook hands with Ray Ebsen. And Mr. Delaney hung around behind Mom, looking goony.

It was too gross for words.

While they patched things up, I headed back up to the top of Chicken Liver Hill, where Brian was still hanging out with the girls. I had a few things to patch up, too.

From the top of the hill, everything looked far away. The adults stood in a little knot. Then I saw Sweetie Pie running through the parking lot, heading toward the food tables. I could hear her happy, dopey bark all the way up here.

Mom and Mr. Delaney broke away from the crowd. They got hot chocolates and stood sipping them, talking. Great. Now my mom was going to start dating my homeroom teacher? That was almost as bad as being haunted by a ghost!

"Thanks a lot, Buddy," I muttered.

"Don't mention it, kid," Buddy said.

I jumped. "Stop doing that!"

To my surprise, Buddy looked the way he did the first time I'd seen him. Not good, you understand. But more like a plain ordinary ghost instead of a decomposing one.

Buddy turned so I could see his profile. "Like it?"

"How come? What happened? Why aren't you, uh, gross like before?" I asked.

"I just wanted to put a little pressure on you, kid," Buddy said. "I thought maybe you were starting to like having me around."

"Oh, yeah, I love having you around," I said. "*Not.*"

Buddy laughed and looked down at the parking lot. "What a crew," he said, shaking his head. "Haven't changed a bit."

"Wait a second, Buddy," I said. "Were you the one who put Elsie Toomer's memento box in with the rummage sale things?"

"I always said you were smart," Buddy said. "A tad on the cube side, but you're improving."

"But why?" I asked. "If you knew Elsie took your ID, you knew she was the one who overheard the fight...Hold on. Were you afraid she tampered with your brakes? To protect the chief? Or because she was jealous of Chi Chi—I mean, Mom?" I clutched my head. "I'm so confused. Why did you tell me you thought the chief was the murderer?"

"I never said I was murdered, kid."

"*What?*"

"I didn't say it." Buddy pointed to me. "*You* did."

"But you said you had to come back and make things right."

"*Exactamente.*" Buddy waved down at the parking lot. "Do I do good work, or what?"

"But you said that you didn't cut your own brake cable."

"And I didn't. I knew my car was worked on in shop that day. Mr. Zambezi, the shop teacher, told me. I forgot. It was my own fault I crashed into that tree. But I didn't want people to go around thinking I did it deliberately! Maybe I wasn't too smart, sure. But I was no coward."

"Wait a second," I said. "You definitely said you came back for revenge."

"So I stretched the truth a little bit. Sue me." Buddy shrugged and gave that white-gummed grimace that passed for a smile. "What I also said was, somebody wasn't letting me rest in peace. That was true. Somebody was feeling so guilty

119

her whole life that she was scared of making one false move. She was always thinking disaster was around every corner."

"Are you talking about Mom?" I said slowly.

Buddy nodded.

"You mean you knew all along that Mom was Chi Chi?"

Buddy shrugged.

"And you came back to *help* her?"

Buddy nodded. "And clear my good name." He jerked his chin toward the church parking lot. "Gerry isn't really good enough for her, but let's face it, I'm the only one who is. And I don't think your mom would be too crazy about me moving in with you guys, you know?"

"She's not the only one," I said.

"You've got a real obnoxious streak, you know that, kid?" Buddy said.

"Well," I said, "I guess you had to come back. But I wish you didn't have to scare me so much."

"Part of my job description," Buddy said. "Besides, you never wimped out, right?"

I thought about it. "No," I said slowly. "I guess I didn't."

"There's a reason why you ended up in the Shadow Zone, kid. Not everybody can handle the place, but you had the right stuff."

Just then, I saw Brian trudging up the hill. "Careful," I said to Buddy. "Here comes Brian."

"No problemo, kid. It's happy-trail time. I gotta make like a banana and split. Take care of your mom for me. And be cool, Toby Bernard Bemus."

Bernard. That was Buddy's name!

"Hey," I said. "Did Mom name me after—" But Buddy only smiled and faded away.

In another minute, Brian rounded the pine tree and came up to me.

"Greetings," I said.

"Who was that guy you were talking to?"

"What guy?" I said.

"The guy in the black leather jacket. Wasn't he cold? He wasn't wearing gloves or anything. Where'd he go, anyway?" Brian looked all around, but the hill was deserted.

"You saw him?" I said. "You saw Buddy?"

Brian frowned. "Don't start that again, Toby. Geez. Haven't you tried to make a fool of me enough this week?"

Then I heard laughing. It was a Buddy laugh, echoing and ghostly.

Brian's freckles stood out against his white face. "Did you hear that?"

I nodded.

"Wait a second," Brian said. He looked really

scared. The sun went behind a cloud. He shivered. "That didn't sound like the wind."

"You're right. It was Buddy. Brian, listen. How do you think I got around that tree before?" I asked him. "You know I'm a Chicken Liver. Buddy helped me."

Brian sat down hard in the snow. "I don't believe I'm believing this," he said. He rubbed his face with his gloved hand. "I mean, I don't know *what* to believe. Ghosts? That's crazy."

"Well, it's all over anyway," I said. "Buddy just said good-bye."

I reached down to help Brian up. When you're wearing two sweaters and a ski jacket, sometimes you *need* a hand. We started down the back side of Chicken Liver Hill.

"Now I'll never know the truth," Brian said.

Suddenly there was a voice in my ear. "Hey, kid, go by the Wilkerson place on the way home," Buddy said. "Old Man Wilkerson fell down the stairs fifty years ago and broke his neck. He's still complaining about it." Then he laughed again.

Brian stopped and whipped his head around. "This is so *weird*," he said.

"Remember, Toby," Buddy whispered in my ear. "The Shadow Zone is always only a half step away."

Then he was gone for good. I don't know how I knew, but I knew.

"Let's head home," Brian said with a shudder. "It's getting dark."

"Sure," I said. "But I have an idea. Let's go by the old Wilkerson place..."

Don't miss the next book in the
Shadow Zone series:
GUESS WHO'S DATING A WEREWOLF?

"Jake is here already," I whispered to Lily.

Creeping up the hill, we crouched low in the underbrush. The full moon showered him with light, making it easy for us to see him as he paced back and forth. He raked his curly hair back nervously, and I felt sorry for him.

"I wonder if Sara stood him up," I whispered.

"She wouldn't dare," Lily murmured.

But I wasn't so sure. My sister had a selfish streak. Had she given up on Jake already? Was he pacing because his heart was broken?

Longing for the truth, I studied Jake's face. His jaw was clenched tightly, and his skin seemed to simmer in the heat.

"I think he's sick," said Lily.

He looked weak, as if he was going to pass out. "Maybe we should help—." But before I could finish the sentence, the most terrible thing began to happen...